AFTER ISAAC

AVRA WING

ISBN: 0615669468
ISBN 13: 9780615669465

Library of Congress Control Number: 2012912649
Published by Olinville Press
New York, New York

ACKNOWLEDGEMENTS

I want to thank all those who helped me while writing this book. First, my husband, Mike Wing, for many things, but, suffice it to say here, for his expert editing. Then, Sarah Crowe, who believed in the book. Ellen Peixoto, for her eagle eye and crucial suggestions. Beth Umland, who generously agreed to look over the manuscript several times and substantially improved it. Rachel Wing, who took the time to read and re-read it, for her insight. Eli Wing, for his linguistic guidance. Susan Shapiro, for all her advice over the years. Laura Anne Gilman, for pointing me in the right direction. And heartfelt thanks to the remarkable families who graciously shared their stories with me.

1

THE WOULD-BE GREAT ESCAPE ARTIST

So here I am, on a bus in the middle of China in the middle of the night. This is one trip I never thought I'd take. It's so weird really—I was The Would-Be Great Escape Artist, and now I have escaped. We all have: Mom, Dad and me. No question we're in a whole other place. We've come a long, long way. And I don't mean just miles and time zones.

Sitting here, looking out the window, we're imagining what's coming next. Actually looking forward to something. I have to tell you, there was a time I thought that could never be. Not after what we'd been through the last three years. Not after Isaac.

I was thirteen when it happened. In the year that followed I was in a really bad way. Spending way too much time alone in my room. Our room. The room I had shared with my brother, down on the ground floor of our house. All his stuff was still there, on the other side of the divider, in Isaac's half. Everything was how he left it—his video games, action figures, even the dirty clothes. I used to drive myself crazy thinking I heard something, like Isaac getting up from bed or maybe turning in his sleep. I'd forget, for a second or two, that he wasn't alive.

I would sit on the floor, leaning against the bed, staring out at the backyard at the skinny tree in the center. What is it called? I can never remember. And those purple flowers popping their heads out of the ground like they did every spring. As if nothing had changed. Same old room, same old yard, same old me, Aaron Saturn. Except it wasn't quite me anymore.

The last thing I wanted to do was go upstairs and "say hello" to the people Mom and Dad were always inviting over. It seemed every weekend they had some new friends visiting. The "company," they would call them. They suddenly knew so many people, always filling up the house, Mom fussing over what to give them to eat. Where did all those people come from? How did they even meet so many people?

It used to be they had, maybe, two, three couples they hung around with. Mostly the parents of kids who were my friends, or Isaac's. Of course, after, they didn't want to see the parents of Isaac's friends anymore. How could they stand it? It's bad enough running into them on the street—or seeing his friends getting bigger, doing all the things Isaac will never get to do.

I'd pop my earphones in so I couldn't hear Mom or Dad calling me to come upstairs to talk to whoever was there visiting, or I'd make up some excuse. I mean, what would I say to them, anyway?

I didn't want to see anybody—not even good old Sam, even though we've been best friends since kindergarten. The only okay thing about having company was that the house wasn't as quiet. All that silence was creepy.

Sometimes I felt like I couldn't even move my body, or that when I did I was passing through something thick—like the agar we used in bio class. Like in a dream where you want to raise your arm, but it just doesn't happen. Other times it was as if I was floating in space and never quite touching the ground.

And when I would finally drag over my backpack and take out all the overdue homework assignments, all I could do was stare at them awhile: Math. French. Global. My first year of high school and not much to show for it. I wound up stuffing the papers back in. Couldn't do shit. Me, the "big brain"—the one who always got As. Didn't even have the energy to play the Wii. Zombie Boy: That was me.

I would get wild ideas about getting away. Out of Brooklyn, out of New York City. *Somewhere else.*

I would think about the places the four of us had gone to on vacation. Maine was the best. Those summers we rented a cottage on Long Lake. Getting up early to hear the insane noise of the loons. And I loved to watch the mist rise off the water. I even wrote a cheesy poem about that, some bullshit about the mist being dreams lifting into the sky. And then, with the sun up, we would dive into the icy lake and race to the raft. The two of us. Damn, it was cold! Laughing like a couple of idiots, we would pull ourselves up out of the water. Me and Isaac.

Yeah, right. Going back to Maine was a genius idea. It would hurt way too much to be there again. So I tried to imagine a place he never was. Where nobody knew what had happened. Where everything didn't remind me of Isaac.

Sometimes I thought maybe Italy. Cousin Lil—she was actually Mom's cousin—used to talk about it a lot, about wanting to go back there. I think that was where she'd been happiest in her life, the way she went on about the art, the food, the people. All the times she tried to show me books of the art in Venice, Florence, Rome, or drag me to the museum, but I never paid much attention. All I knew about Italy, except for reading *Julius Caesar* in seventh grade, was that the guys at the pizzeria were all from there.

Lil. I know Mom took it hard when she died. Of course, it was nothing like what happened with Isaac. Lil was pretty old, a lot older than Mom, and sick. We thought we knew what sad was when she passed.

But we were wrong.

2

NICER THAN MOST

As many times as I go over it, it'll never make any sense. We were just back at school, so it had to be after Thanksgiving break. A Wednesday. No, a Thursday. Or maybe it *was* a Wednesday. I still can't remember what classes I had that day. It was just a regular day. No sign. Nothing to let us know. Me and Isaac went to school together, just like always. Unless one of us was sick. But Isaac was hardly ever sick! He'd just grown a couple of inches, and his pants were too short. His socks showed beneath the bottom of his jeans. He looked so ridiculous! But he didn't care. What eleven-year-old boy gives a shit about what he's wearing?

Not that he was a typical kid. He was nicer than most people. Like that morning on the way to the D train, even though we were already late, Isaac had to stop to hand a dollar to a homeless guy, and then, of course, I had to give Isaac more money so he'd have enough for lunch. And then when we got down into the station and Isaac realized he'd forgotten his MetroCard, I got so mad at him. I guess I could be pretty much of a dick sometimes.

I remember him waiting for me after school on the stairs in the lobby, just like always. He was sketching. He loved to draw—people, mostly. He was looking pretty shaggy, his dark hair over his eyes.

What did we talk about on the train going home? *Why can't I remember?* I think we went into Video Forum. It was still there then. Isaac had pretty good taste in movies for a kid. He was just getting into Hitchcock.

And then what did we do? Waste our time playing some video game? Probably. Did homework. Ate dinner. Isaac kept talking about getting a dog from that guy on the street, the one we call Crazy Harold. Mom didn't want to, but Dad was caving. Then we watched TV. Some stupid show. *Lost*, maybe. And then we just went to bed. Like any other night. Mom kissed us and said she'd see us bright and early for school in the morning. But there was no morning for Isaac. Sometime, in the night, his heart stopped.

Had he cried out? Did I sleep through it? Could I have done something to save him? Everybody told me it must have happened very fast and quietly, no way I would have heard something, no chance to help. Still, there were times I couldn't stop thinking about it, telling myself it was my fault. So I had to get out of the house and go somewhere that Saturday, that first time

I snuck away. I lied to Mom and Dad, which was a shitty thing to do.

"Mom? Dad? I'm going out for a while," I called up to them, trying to act casual.

"Where, Aaron? Where are you going?" Mom yelled back.

She sounded worried, but if I went up and faced her I knew I'd never get away.

"I don't know. Just a walk."

"By yourself? For how long?"

They never used to question me like that. They used to trust me to go to the movies or a store or for pizza, even into Manhattan, without asking for every detail. I knew what was behind it. They were afraid I'd get hurt, maybe even killed. Or just disappear. Then they'd be down to zero kids. So I made up something to calm them.

"I'm going to the bookstore. Just to look around."

"Why don't you come up a bit first? The Millers are here."

"Oh." I made my voice a bit louder, as if I were trying to talk to the Millers, whoever the hell they were. "Hi. How are you? Mom … can I go? Is it okay?"

No answer. I guessed Mom and Dad were exchanging looks. They did that a lot those days—checking out each other's reactions, always trying to say and do the right thing, always doubting themselves.

"Yes. Of course," Dad said, but I remember he sounded pretty reluctant. Then Mom said, "Don't be gone too long. Take an umbrella. It looks like it's going to start raining again."

I grabbed my jacket and left without the umbrella. Once I was outside, I felt like I could breathe again. The air was so fresh; it had that clean rainy smell. It smelled like spring. But before I started to feel all happy, I reminded myself that Isaac wouldn't be around to enjoy it.

I walked along Seventh Avenue. Everything was the same. Somehow my brother had died, but the rest of the world just kept on. The same stores—GameStop, Little Things, D'Vine Taste. The same places to eat—Pino's, Shinju, Two Boots. I stopped in front of the firehouse to look at the memorial that was there all those years since 9/11. A lot of their guys died that day, all at once. And people started leaving out bunches of flowers and candles. Still do.

The father of a kid in my class was one of the fire-fighters who was killed. I didn't understand anything about it then. I mean I was what—six? In first grade or something. But after we lost Isaac, I went by the fire-house a lot.

If something so unbelievable like the Towers being destroyed could happen, well, maybe it's not so strange that a kid could die. Anything was possible. I didn't get it until Isaac was gone—that you just never knew what was next. That's what people must have felt that day.

It was a time the whole world—*kapow*—had been as off-balance as I was.

3

TODAY MY NAME IS KIM

I had no idea where I was going. I told Mom and Dad I was headed for the bookstore just to say something. I found myself walking toward the subway. It's really gross down there. Stinks from piss. Garbage on the tracks. Rats too. But if you want to get anywhere in the City, it's the way to go. Whenever we went to Natural History or Coney Island or wherever, we took the train. Me and Isaac would get all excited when we heard the train screeching into the station and saw the lights as the first car turned the corner. Sometimes we would even fight over who spotted it first, who was the first one to see the lights, see the front of the train. How lame was that?

I stood at the very edge of the platform, on the bumpy, bright-yellow warning strip. I guess they made it uneven like that so even blind people could feel it with their canes and get the message: don't go past this line. But it was tempting, believe me. I thought about inching my toes over the edge until I fell onto the tracks. Did I mention I was in a bad way? But I knew I couldn't do that to Mom and Dad. Couldn't take it that far.

I grabbed a seat and tried to think about where to go as the stations flicked by: Fourth Avenue, Smith–Ninth, Carroll, Bergen, Jay, and then the extra beat while we crossed into Manhattan: East Broadway, Delancey, Second Avenue, Broadway–Lafayette. That last one sounded familiar. I'd gone there with Sam a couple of times, so I got out.

I decided to try to find the places we'd been to, although it wouldn't be the same without Sam. We are so different, but we've managed to stay friends for a long time. I remember when I first met him in kindergarten. It must have been a "free time" when we weren't learning to write our names with all the letters facing the right way, or trying to wrap our tiny brains around the whole days/weeks/months thing. There was a bunch of kids crowded into the housekeeping corner, and in the middle of them was Sam. He was being the Daddy. He was reading to the Baby. Some animal story. Probably he was pretending to read. But he was doing different voices for the pig and goat and cow and whatever. And all these other kids were, like, mesmerized. And that was it. I knew that kid was going to be my BFF.

I wandered around until I found Other Music and looked through some of the imports, stuff it's hard to get even on the Net, then browsed through the T-shirts in Yellow Rat Bastard. I guess they were supposed to be all hip, with Japanese words and anime characters on them. The whole time I was thinking that Mom and Dad would be freaked when they realized how long I'd been gone. And I didn't care. I even turned off my cell so they couldn't bug me every two minutes.

The streets were pretty full—NYU students, bunches of tourists, kids my age in groups of three or four, Chinese grandmothers with babies strapped to their backs. I walked uptown. There was a crowd of grungy men playing chess at the stone tables in Washington Square. They looked kind of damp, like they had played right through the rain. As I got closer to St. Mark's Place, I started to see East Village-types with spiked, dyed hair wearing black, black, and more black, and some street people asleep in doorways, curled up in their rags. I remember there was a guy eating something out of a garbage can. And a man on Avenue C standing over a blanket piled with all sorts of junk, trying to sell it. Greasy, bent hats. Broken appliance motors. Chipped dishes. I was a kid with only a few bucks in my pocket, but I was way ahead of the game.

It started to rain hard, and I ducked into a bookstore. So I actually did wind up in a bookstore! The art books were out front. Lil would have been happy. She had tried to get us interested in drawing and painting and like that. Isaac was. He could have been an artist, just like she was. He really had talent. But Lil never made me feel like I was an asshole or anything for not being into it. It was great that she lived right across the street. It made things more special somehow—Mom always inviting her over, or us going to Lil's for some holiday or other. I miss Thanksgiving at Lil's with her artist friends and their stories about all the famous people like Warhol they used to hang with, or the crazy things they used to do when they were young and drunk. Or about how great New York was years ago, how they missed all these old-timey places in Greenwich Village that aren't there anymore. And then they'd argue over who was or wasn't a great painter. I couldn't always follow what they were talking about, but it was still fun.

I guess Lil wasn't really famous, but she sold her work, mostly oils of city scenes. They were good. Not that I'd know. But I liked them. Really looked like the buildings and streets. And the old canal, the Gowanus, that runs along the edge of our neighborhood. Sometimes we'd all go to the opening night parties of her work in these tiny galleries in Brooklyn or Manhattan. Me and Isaac spent the whole time picking out the grapes and strawberries from the fruit platters.

I started looking through the books. I noticed one called something like *A Survey of Chinese Painting and Pottery*. Strange, right? Maybe I had a feeling—? On the cover were all these clay soldier guys in rows. I mean a lot of them, just stretching on and on. Inside it explained that they were the terra cotta warriors of Xi'an lined up in a tomb. Some emperor thought that after he died he'd need an army in heaven! That he would still be in charge, and that the mud people would come to life and march around protecting him.

I looked at other pictures of funny old men with big heads wearing robes. And one of a kind of palace with people around it doing different things—just taking a walk, eating, playing music. It was peaceful, but the bad thoughts kept getting in the way. Like how Mom's face looked that morning when she understood Isaac was dead.

I put down the book and rushed out of the store and was headed for Forbidden Planet to check out the comics when this girl came up to me.

"Hey, man, got any change?"

"Huh?"

She was really thin, her hair filthy. She looked around my age, fourteen or so. She was soaked! Probably had been out in the rain for a while.

"I don't have much on me," I told her. I had just one fare left on my MetroCard and a little money for some food.

"NBD."

I don't know what got into me. I don't usually talk to strangers. Especially strung-out ones. I just wanted to talk to her, though.

"How come you're out here begging? Don't you have a home or something?" It was like I suddenly cared.

She didn't answer that, just said, kind of annoyed, "Oh, dude, I don't want no heart-to-heart. I could use some extra money is all."

"Sorry." Neither of us moved. We just stared at each other for a second.

Then, just like that, she asked, "So, you wanna chill? I know some people over on East Third."

I was so surprised I didn't say anything. She took that as a no.

"Hey, it's cool. You think maybe it'll get weird. No way. Those people make me sick. Someone took me to one of those places once. You wouldn't believe it. They wear leather ... everywhere."

I didn't know what the hell she was talking about. I said something really profound like, "Ah, I see."

"So, you coming? Beats being alone. You're alone, you hear yourself think. Who needs that? I don't want to hear the noise going on inside my head. I'd rather talk to somebody else, even if they got nothing to say, you know? I meet all sorts of people that way."

"Like those people you're going to see?"

"Not really. They're Spanish, man. No English. Can't talk to *them*. But they're okay. They always let me stay awhile."

"How did you meet them if you can't talk to each other?"

She looked at me as if she couldn't believe anyone could say something so stupid.

"This guy, Carlo? Works in the movie theater on Second Avenue. You know the one? Seven floors, man. You can go in there and get lost and see movies all day. So this guy? He liked my friend Yolanda. Well, she *was* my friend. And he snuck us in 'cause nobody cares, and then we met *his* friend and went back to the friend's place and his sister was there and my friend changed her mind and they got mad but the sister was sick and I gave her my coat."

It took me a minute to figure that one out: movies, Yolanda, sister, coat. "Did your parents give you a hard time when you came home without your coat?"

"What do you mean?"

"Like, was your mother angry?"

She thought that was HI-sterical, just about doubled over. "My mother? Oh my God, I don't even know where she is!"

I didn't find that too funny. Just the opposite. "Really? How come?"

14

The girl didn't answer. Clearly this was off limits. Instead, I asked her, "And how's the sister?"

"Bad, man."

"What's she have?"

"How do I know? Do I look like a fuckin' doctor?"

"I just thought—"

"People die, man." She shrugged. "The brother, he knows she's going to die. So he keeps the house nice. He keeps it nice for her. Rosa. She's his only family. The Spanish care about that family stuff."

"Everybody cares about that."

"Not me, man. If I did, I'd really be crazy. I don't stay with my parents no more. It was all fucked up."

"Why?"

"I ain't telling you my private business," she said, turning away.

I didn't want her to leave, so I said, "By the way, what's your name?" She looked back at me and, no longer annoyed, gave me a big smile.

"Today my name is Kim. Like that actress. Kim Novak?"

"Right. The one in the Hitchcock movies."

"Whatever. My grandma had these old postcards she used to collect when she was a little, little kid, from chewing gum? *The Hollywood Stars*, something like that. Really old. I mean black and white! But they still smelled like bubble gum. Sometimes I would sneak a look at them. And that's where I saw the picture. Kim Novak. I kind of look like her."

It was mean, but I almost said, "On a really bad day." Instead, I agreed, "Yeah. Kind of." She seemed pleased. Then, not that she'd asked, I told her, "My name is Aaron. Today and every day."

She wanted to know if I was coming with her to Carlo's. I thought about it, but it was like I couldn't move.

"I get it. You're worried maybe you'll catch something from Rosa? It's cool. You gotta keep your health, right?"

It made me almost want to take the chance. I remember having the idea—*I could get sick and die.*

"Me, I don't care," she said. "Nothing won't happen to me. I got my saints to protect me. They make me a magic circle. A life-force all around me. The lady in the *botánica* set it up."

It didn't sound any more insane than a mud army for a dead emperor. All I said was something like, "Uh-huh," but Kim thought I was making fun of her.

"You think that's bullshit, but it's true."

"Could be," I said. I mean, what do I know?

Then she asked if maybe I didn't have something to give her. "For Rosa?"

I realized that Isaac would have given her something right away. I handed over some change.

"I'll tell Rosa about you," she said, taking it.

"It'll be a short conversation," I joked.

Kim laughed.

Then I said, "Tell Rosa I hope she gets better. I hope she lives."

After she walked away I felt exhausted, as if talking to her had taken all my energy. I bought a cheap slice, wolfed it down, and headed back to the subway. I was going to have to face Mom and Dad, but there was nothing to do but get back home.

4

A LITTLE SHORT IN THE LUCK DEPARTMENT

Mom and Dad were on me the second they heard the downstairs gate open.

"Aaron! We were worried sick," Mom said. "We didn't know what happened to you! How could you do that to us? What is wrong with you? Look at you— you're soaked! You said you wouldn't be gone long and it's been over three hours! Why didn't you answer your phone?"

Dad stood back a little, softly telling Mom to let it go.

I could see Mom's eyes were kind of puffy and red and I felt really bad. I tried to explain. "I'm sorry, Mom. I just had to get away. I know it was dumb. Nothing happened. I just got on the subway and went a few stops into the City."

That got her even more upset. Even Dad looked like he was going to pass out or something, leaning against the wall like he needed the support. Suddenly, crossing over the bridge into Manhattan was an epic thing. He said something lame like, "Next time, just tell us, okay?"

Things were pretty tense for the week after that. I went to school, Mom went to work at her day care, Dad did—I don't know. He would go into the room he used as his study, where he kept all his records for his contracting business, and disappear for a few hours. Sometimes I heard him on the phone. Maybe he was staying in touch with his workmen. We all ate dinner together, but didn't say much.

Mom and Dad seemed to be calming down about it, but I realized it was because they had just kicked the whole thing over to my shrink. I had started seeing Dr. Orbach a few months after Isaac died. Mom and Dad made me. At first I barely opened my mouth during our sessions. I didn't feel like telling anything to this guy I didn't know. But after a while, I started saying some stuff. When I got to his office on Saturday, he brought up my disappearing act right away.

"You had your parents very worried."

I looked at Orbach sitting there in his leather armchair, waiting for me to talk. I think he's an okay guy; I even thought so then. But I didn't want to hear any lectures. So I told him it wasn't my fault if they were so frantic all the time. "If I drop dead like Isaac, there's nothing they can do about it, anyway," I said. I guess I had an attitude.

"That's true. And that's just it. Because of what happened they feel helpless. Scared."

I knew that—and that I had done something to make them more scared. And that part of me hadn't cared.

"So let's try to understand why you did it."

I was so tired of thinking through everything I did—or didn't do. I just wanted to sit there, my mind blank. I looked away from Orbach, glanced at the posters on the wall from Tanglewood, the music festival. One was a photograph of a crowd on the lawn. Orbach once told me he's in it, somewhere in the middle, sitting on a blanket. The day someone took that picture must have been a good day for him. Then, just to look at something else and not at Orbach, I stared down at his rug. I had always wondered about the design. It looked like some kind of Chinese writing. I asked him if it meant anything.

He told me it was a Chinese "character" doubled up next to itself. Pronounced "she" but in English it would be spelled *xi*. Weird. It's supposed to mean good luck, happiness. It made sense to me that you would need two. One might not be enough. You could never be too sure.

"Do you think the good luck will rub off on your patients?" I was being a sarcastic schmuck, but he actually said yes.

"Something like that. I want to set up a feeling of hope."

"Well, it's not working."

But the whole Chinese thing made me think about the day in Manhattan, the art book and the mud men.

I found myself telling him about Kim. How she seemed to be living on the street. How she seemed to be a little short in the luck department. And how for a second there I had thought about going with her.

"Why didn't you?"

"I don't know. It was like I was paralyzed or something."

That's mostly what I felt those days. Numb. Like I was that kid they made that old movie about who had to live in a bubble and life was going on outside the bubble. Like nothing was quite real—school, people, me. Sometimes I had the crazy thought that Isaac hadn't been real. Maybe I had imagined having a brother.

But then the next minute I would think that the unreal part was his dying. That it had all been a bad dream. And that when I got home, Isaac would be sitting on his bed, iPod in, eating Skittles. I mean it was too insane that he had died. How could someone—a kid, a kid like any other kid, who had an orange backpack, who left dirty clothes piled up in his room, who liked karate and hated soccer, who could draw and was good in English but lousy at math, who had once taken a pack of Sour Straws from a bodega and felt awful about it for weeks, who had his own smell and a favorite pair of jeans—just not be alive anymore? And no one exactly knew why? His heart had just stopped? He hadn't even been sick! He was alive watching TV the evening before, and then sometime in the middle of the night, when I was sleeping in the room with him, he had died.

When my hour with Orbach was over I went out to Mom who was sitting in the waiting room. I didn't understand why she insisted on coming with me to my appointments. She would just hang there reading one of the old magazines Orbach kept. I guess it was stuff that kept her mind off Isaac. Like Orbach knew what waiting moms who just had a kid die wanted to read.

I was always a little anxious to get the hell out of there because this little boy, Owen, who I thought was kind of strange, came in after me, and I didn't want to get stuck talking to him. He always came up too close and touched me. There was something creepy about him. I mean, I know kids. I see them all the time at Mom's nursery school, and I knew that Owen, who must have been about seven then, was too old to act that way. But Mom held up a copy of *People* or some such and said she just needed a minute to finish reading an article.

Sure enough, the next second Owen came running through the door, followed by his nutso mother, who's always telling him what to do. He came right up to me, shouting my name way too loud. Asking me if I liked Yu-Gi-Oh, if I wanted to see his Yu-Gi-Oh cards.

"Owen, you're bothering that boy," his mother said. So of course I had to say it was okay, just to get in her face.

She went on and on about didn't he remember that they had had a whole thing about his talking too much? And all I could think was that *she* talked too much.

Then Owen said, "The teacher too. She said I couldn't control myself. She didn't like it. My talking all the time. So they put me in a special school. I don't care. Nobody liked me at my old school, anyway."

Owen's mother started to rub the sides of her head as if she was getting a headache.

I felt bad for the kid so I said something like, "It can be hard in a new school." I sounded like Mister-Fucking-Rogers.

Then he asked me, "Aaron, you crazy too? Is that why you come here?"

I had to laugh. But both Mom and Owen's mother looked as if their eyes were going to pop.

Owen's mother started babbling some apology. "He doesn't know what he's saying half the time. He just talks. No one here is crazy."

"The kids say I must be to have a si-ki-a-trist." Owen said the word very slowly, making sure he got it right.

So I figured what the hell, and told him I guess I was crazy too.

"It's like a club," he said, all happy. "The Crazy Club. The Owen and Aaron Crazy Club."

And the kid gave me a big smile—and I actually felt pretty good there for a second.

5

GO, GATORS

Mom and I walked out of the apartment house where Orbach had his office and started home. There aren't a lot of these taller buildings in our neighborhood. Mainly it's three- and four-story houses made of wood or brownstone or brick built like a hundred years ago. Dad loves these old places. He's always talking about their details—wood floors and plaster moldings and like that. I guess they're okay.

It was a nice day, sunny and the temperature just right. I remember looking around and seeing that every other house seemed to be having a stoop sale. People had their stuff lined up on their front steps, with clothes hanging from the cast-iron fences. It was nicer than the shit I saw on Avenue C, that's for sure. Lots of toys, children's bikes, vinyl LPs, books. Families getting rid of things their kids had outgrown, or stuff they'd gotten tired of. Just like the leaves and flowers start coming out in spring—people's old junk was in season.

Mom and Lil used to go to the sales a lot. So I asked Mom if she wanted to stop at any of them. But she hadn't even noticed. She gave me this sad smile. "It's so funny. When we'd be walking together and I or Lil wanted to go to those you and ... Isaac would groan and beg us not to. And now Isaac's ... gone ... and Lil's ... gone ... and you're asking me if I want to go to a stoop sale."

Yeah, it was definitely fucked up. But I wouldn't have minded stopping that day. Anything but go home. Weekdays were bad enough, with everyone at school checking me out to see if I was going to cry or explode. But Saturday and Sunday were endless.

As we went by a house with a table of books in front, Mom sort of glanced at them, but kept going. A block later we reached the flea market held in the schoolyard in the middle of Seventh Avenue every weekend. Mom looked it over. "I haven't been here since I sold some of Lil's jewelry after she died," she remembered. Then she added, "You were kind of mad at me for doing that."

I told her it didn't matter. But, when it happened, I was really pissed. It seemed wrong, although I don't know what else she could have done. Even after Mom kept some of the stuff, there was still a ton more bracelets and pins and whatever. Lil had left almost everything to Mom. I guess since Lil had been an only child and she'd never married or had kids, Mom was almost like a sister or daughter to her.

Mom had made a few hundred bucks, and we wound up giving the money to Crazy Harold, the weird guy who wore the same clothes all the time and stood in front of the laundromat to get donations to help the stray dogs he took in. And those are some sorry-looking animals.

Lil had liked him for some reason. She always spoke to him and gave him a few dollars every week. She said it was a blessing what he did for those dogs. And the funniest part was that she didn't even like dogs that much. When he heard what the money we gave him was from, he was sad. He said Lil had been such a nice lady, even though she'd never take a dog. And then, without missing a beat, he asked if we wanted one. That had gotten Isaac started on the dog thing.

We went into the schoolyard, and I followed Mom around for a while. There were a lot of people and piles of used furniture, old rugs, ugly paintings of skylines and farm animals and flowers. She didn't spend much time on anything until we reached a table in the back where a pretty Chinese woman was sitting. Mom began to look at the bottles and statues and necklaces that were laid out on a table, asking about them, and I began to feel like an idiot. I didn't want to go home, but I didn't want to stand there, either.

Mom picked up that I was really uncomfortable. So she suggested—not for the first time—that I walk over to the park and practice with my baseball team. I had quit going since Isaac died. Had missed a whole season and was out of shape. Before, I had liked it a lot. Wasn't half bad, either. Isaac never liked team sports. He didn't get it—the excitement standing at home plate, bat ready, watching the pitch zoom closer, hoping to get a hit. It just made him nervous.

"Baseball's a waste," I told her.

"You didn't used to think so."

"I didn't used to think a lot of things," I said.

Mom ignored that remark.

"Dad went out of his way to stay in touch with your coach, you know. And not just Larry—other people in the league, to make sure they wouldn't drop you from the team."

"I'm *so* grateful Dad made some phone calls." I had a smart answer for everything. It was tough on Mom, how she had to manage to keep calm and not react to my being angry all the time.

All she said was that she and Dad were busy later that afternoon, anyway. They were going to be seeing the Millers again. They're the people, I found out, that Mom and Dad met in a grief support group. Their son died from cancer. I didn't really know them then or realize that they would, in a way, have an effect on my life. She asked if I wanted to go with them all to the museum instead.

"Actually, they're interesting people," Mom said like she was trying to sell me something. "She's an artist. Does these woodcuts. Very strong work. Reminds me a little of Lil's. And he's a professor. History. He's always got an unusual take on politics. And they know how to talk to us. I hate it when everyone's always walking on eggshells around us. 'Oh, we should be nice to poor Claire and Barry.' With Jim and Grace we can relax."

Well, relaxing in some museum and talking about dead children did not seem like a great way to spend an afternoon. To get out of it, I decided that showing up for practice wasn't such a bad idea.

I felt a little guilty, though, going off to do something sort of fun. But Mom kept telling me it was okay.

So I said I would just see what the old Gators were up to. Just to check it out. I even had the thought that maybe Mom had decided to hang at the market just to make me so bored I would have no choice but to go.

I walked uphill to the park and past the stone lions or tigers or whatever they are guarding the Third Street entrance. There were little kids in the playground, people on the grass throwing around Frisbees, runners and cyclists on the paths. The park looked pretty good with the bare tree branches starting to fill out with leaves.

I spotted Larry, my coach, as soon as I got near the ball fields. He's so tall you can see him a mile away. When I got up closer all he said was, "Well, well, well, if it isn't my third baseman deciding to report to practice." At least Larry knew not to make a big deal about things. He wasn't the walking-on-eggshells-type. Didn't say a word about how long I'd been gone—or why.

I asked how he'd been.

"Me? I'm fine. But you … late." Then he looked me over and said, pretending to be annoyed, "Without a mitt. Or hat." He tossed me an old glove, and I joined the kids who were fielding balls hit by the other half of the team. Everyone just nodded at me. One or two gave me a "Sup?" I hadn't seen some of them since they'd come to Isaac's funeral. They hadn't even looked like themselves in dress-up clothes. Now here we all were. Isaac was dead, and I was playing ball again. Going for a grounder.

"Good pickup, Aaron," Larry shouted. "That's the way."

Isaac would have teased me—"Oh, he caught a ball!"—and made fun of me for giving a shit about a game. I used to get mad sometimes when he did that, like he was so superior, but I knew even then it was Isaac's twisted way of being proud.

I guess Isaac was something of a klutz. I mean, stuff he could do with his hands—drawing, or even doing things with Dad, fixing things—he was unbelievable at. But when he ran it was as if his arms and legs were going off in ten separate directions. Sort of like a bunch of pinwheels spinning every which way. Funny how we were brothers, but totally different people. Maybe that's why we got along pretty well. We didn't need to step on each other's strong points. I'm not saying it was perfect—that there weren't times I called him horrible names when he got on my nerves, or times when he got so mad at me for going after him that he'd start punching.

That first day back, I just got into it: shagging grounders, BP, wind sprints. It was good to be sweaty and tired and not think about anything.

"Remember, there's only two more weeks until our first game, gentlemen," Larry shouted to us as practice broke up. "We play on Field Number Three at nine a.m., and you are to be there an hour before the game, *in uniform*! And tell your parents to get you cleats already."

As I was leaving, Sean, our pitcher, called to me. "Some of the guys are going back to my house. Wanna come?"

I didn't like Sean then. He thought he was all that. Always letting you know what his parents had bought him or when he got an award at school or something— like anyone could care—and going on and on about what a great ball player he was every time he struck someone out. That really went over well. Sometimes I had made fun of him behind his back with the other guys. I'm not proud of it. At least I didn't pull back the skin by my eyes to try to look Chinese-y like some of them did because he's from Korea. But even though they did that, the other guys were more friends with him than I was.

I didn't get it. I couldn't see how people were never letting him forget about being Korean and adopted. Always making him feel different, and not good-different. So, okay, he found ways to build himself up.

Now we're actually kind of friends. But that day, I wasn't ready to chill with him and listen to his bullshit, so I just shook my head.

I still don't like it when people talk big about themselves, make themselves seem important. But I think maybe I have some more idea of why people need to do it. I think I give them more of a break now.

6

TWO SLICES FOR HERE

When I got back home, I headed straight for the kitchen I was so hungry. I stopped, though, when I saw Dad alone in the living room. The TV was on but he wasn't watching. He was looking over a set of house plans spread out on the coffee table and singing some old-timey song softly to himself. It was the one about people handing him hard luck stories that somehow had something to do with saying goodbye to a blackbird. It had never made sense to me. I couldn't remember the last time I'd heard Dad hum or sing. He used to do it a lot—break out in some old song. Or sing us to sleep, the way his father used to do for him.

He looked up when I came into the room. "Hi, there. What have you been up to? You look like you could use a shower."

"I know, right? I went to practice. Baseball. It's a little muddy out there."

"Practice? You went to a baseball practice today? You should have told me. I could have helped out."

"I didn't even decide to go until the last minute. Besides, one or two of the other fathers were there. We were fine."

"Tell me next time, okay?" I could see he was really hurt.

"Sure. Season opens soon."

"Great, great." He stood up to turn off the TV. "How does the team look?"

I made some lame-o joke. "Like a bunch of four-teen-year-old losers." It just slipped out. I mean, jokes seemed off-limits those days. But Dad smiled and didn't look like it bothered him.

I pointed to the plans. "You working, Dad?"

"Sort of." He picked up the papers and held them out for me to look at. "This woman's been calling me for months. I left her house half done. I have Mohammed and Joe finishing it up, but they've hit a snag with the plumbing. I'm just trying to see if there's another way to configure these pipes. Sometimes a quarter-inch can make all the difference."

That's the kind of thing Isaac would have been interested in. I wondered if Dad wished he could talk about it with him instead of me. I was the one who got good grades, but Isaac was the creative one. He liked going on jobs, watching as Dad remade places. If Isaac weren't an artist, he would be an architect. I'd heard Dad and Lil say that more than once.

Then Dad asked if I was hungry and told me Mom wasn't coming home for lunch. That she was still at the flea market. I was really surprised. I had left her there hours ago.

"She called to say she's talking to this Chinese woman or something. You know your mother."

Yeah, I guess I did. Or at least who my mother had become.

I told Dad I was starving and asked if we could go for some pizza.

I think he was about to agree when he said, "Oh, I almost forgot, A-Team, Sam called."

I remember that so well, not so much because of Sam, who had been calling a lot, even though I was always slow to get back to him. But because Dad had used my nickname. Like it was no big deal. It had been awhile since he'd done that. I was A-Team and Isaac was Iz the Whiz.

It made me feel like a little of the fog had lifted.

"I guess I should call Sam back."

"That's up to you."

"Maybe I will."

"Yeah?" Dad seemed glad. He came over and gave me a hug. Then he quickly let go. "Yick, I can't believe I touched your sweaty body."

"I'll wash up and then call Sam."

"That's good. Mom and I are going to see some people later. The Millers."

I don't know what got into me. "The 'interesting' people," I said sarcastically. I was turning into a fucking stand-up.

Dad was happy about it, though. "You're beginning to sound like yourself again," he told me. "Now go clean up, you slob."

I heard Mom come home just as I was stepping out of the shower. Then she and Dad called down that they were going out again.

I punched in Sam's cell number. "Hey, man."

"Hey, Aaron! How are you, dude?"

I knew I didn't have to go into a whole thing for Sam. But I really couldn't tell him how I felt. "Appropriate question. Let's see—totally out of it? But still starving. Wanna go for a slice?"

"Sure. I'll be over in a minute."

It was really great to see skinny old Sam, all six foot two of him. He was wearing one of his typical "conservative" outfits—shiny green pants and a bright orange shirt under a red sweater. Sam's philosophy is that people are going to stare at him anyway—might as well really give them something to look at.

"Hey. Nice duds, Sam. Just let me get my sunglasses."

He looked me over. "And you, as always, are rocking that outfit."

I was, of course, in my own "uniform" of black jeans and untucked button-down shirt. That's about all I ever wear over my slightly plump, five foot nine body.

We went out the downstairs gate and headed for Pino's. Sam started to do a gangsta walk down the sidewalk.

And, for a moment, it was okay, like we were just a couple of guys going for pizza. Well, almost. I felt strange, I told him.

"It feels like I'm watching myself in a movie or something. And that other people are watching me too."

"Like you've landed the role of a troubled teen on ABC Family?"

"Something like that."

"Don't flatter yourself, though. It's the Samster they're looking at."

"Well, maybe. I feel like I've got this smell coming off me. Of bad news."

"Oh, there's a smell all right. But it's more like B.O."

"Oh, really funny."

"At your service." Sam made a bow.

We got to the pizzeria, with its mirrored walls and red plastic booths. No matter what time of day, there's always people there—nannies with little kids climbing over the tables, some cops with their patrol car double-parked outside, an old guy sitting by himself reading the *Post* or *Daily News*.

Jimmy was behind the counter. We've known Jimmy forever. At least since Isaac was a baby in a stroller gumming a pizza crust. I think about how excited me and Isaac had been that first time Mom and Dad let us come here by ourselves. I felt like a big shot, ordering two slices and Hawaiian Punch.

"Okay, boys, what can I do for you?" Jimmy asked, barely looking in our direction.

I ordered our usual, without even having to ask Sam. "Two pepperonis for here." Just what we always had.

Then Jimmy looked up at us to ask if we wanted something to drink. And then he recognized me. "Hey, Aaron. How's it going, man? How's your Mom and Dad doing?"

"You know."

"Yeah. I do." He shook his head. "Let me tell you, since *my* little brother died, well, nothing's the same."

"*Your* brother?" I asked like a jerk.

"Yeah. At the Twin Towers. I never told you?"

Then I remembered and felt even worse. "Sorry. I guess I forgot."

"Doesn't matter. I don't talk too much about it no more, but I thought I told you. Sometimes I think there's something wrong with my head."

"I know what you mean," I agreed.

Then he turned and opened the refrigerated unit that held all the drinks. "Have sodas with that." He handed us two Cokes. "On the house."

He wouldn't let us pay for them. We thanked him and took our food and slid into one of the booths. We started to eat, neither of us talking for a while. Then Sam said, "This world is so fucked up."

It was so good to be back with Sam, who always puts his finger directly on the heart of things.

7

WHO THE HELL IS RAUSCHENBERG?

Sam had brought the latest Zelda with him, and we started to play when we got back to the house. That is the all-time great waste of time. I was just about to pick up an ornamental skull when I heard Mom and Dad come home. I was surprised—I thought they'd be gone awhile. Then Dad called me upstairs in a way that made it sound like I better go pronto.

When I got to the living room and saw their faces, I could tell something was wrong. More than the usual. I started to worry—was one of them sick? Mom looked like she was in a daze.

"Mom? Are you okay? Dad?"

"I was just thinking," he said, not answering me, "why don't we all go to a movie or something?"

That didn't sound so urgent to me. What was going on?

Dad turned to Mom. "Why not, Claire? Let's go out. With Aaron."

She didn't answer.

"Is Sam here?" Dad asked me.

I nodded.

"He could come too. I'm sure there's a film we would all enjoy. What do you say?" He sounded desperate.

"Sure, I guess," I said.

But then Mom spoke. "I don't know," she said, really softly. "I just don't feel up for a movie."

"Well, Claire, let's not sit home. We can still go to the museum. By ourselves. It's open late tonight. Let's go see that Rauschenberg exhibit finally."

"I feel awfully tired, Barry. I'm going to lie down." She left the room and climbed the stairs to their room.

"What's up, Dad?"

"She'll be fine," he said like he didn't believe it was true, and turned to go into the kitchen.

"Did something happen?" I asked as I followed him in.

"No. Not really," he filled a glass with water and took a few sips.

Yeah, right. "Uh, Dad?"

Dad made a face. "You know those people we were visiting? The Millers? You know they also lost a boy a few years back. Well, it seems they're, uh, going to have a baby. Grace is pregnant." He dropped onto a chair at the table.

"Huh?" I couldn't quite grasp it. It made no sense. What did that have to do with Mom? I also thought it was too bizarre that a friend of theirs was going to have a baby; I thought people their age were too old for that sort of thing. "A baby?" I repeated like an idiot.

"Yeah. It's … great. The boy who died——Devin—— was their only child. Now they'll have a child in their lives again."

I mean, a baby is supposed to be a happy thing. But, in this case, something didn't compute. Something seemed wrong. I found myself suddenly getting angry.

"A new kid? Like a substitution? A replacement? They had an opening and decided to fill it with someone else?"

"No, no, of course not," Dad said. "It's not like that. They can't replace the child they lost. It will be a new child, a different child. They want that again. A baby to take care of. They feel they're ready to, that it will be good for them."

"Then why is Mom so upset? Maybe she thinks they're doing something wrong. Maybe she's mad at them."

"I don't think that's it."

"So what is it?"

"I don't know. I don't think *she* even knows." He looked helpless.

"Are *you* upset?" I asked him.

After a moment he said again, "I don't know."

Then a really crazy thought hit me. If the Millers were doing this . . .

"Does *Mom* want a baby? Is that it?"

Dad sighed. "I don't know, Aaron," he repeated. "This just came up. We need time to make sense of it."

The idea got me so weirded out, so mixed up, I felt like a wild animal "Sense? How can you make sense of it? They're going to have this different kid!" I was almost shouting. "So now they can forget about their first kid? If you had a baby, would you forget about Isaac?"

"Aaron! What are you talking about? No, of course not. Nobody's forgetting Isaac. How can you even say that?" He tilted his head up, indicating Mom might overhear us. "Just calm down and lower your voice, will you?"

Dad stood and put his hand on my shoulder and started talking to me again more softly. "It's just so confusing. The Millers are our friends. We wish them well. They have been so kind to us. But now they're moving in another direction. And we don't know if we can follow them there. Or even, to be truthful, be happy for them."

"Are *they* happy?"

"Well. Not so much happy. More like a weight's been lifted off them. It's been a few years and they felt they couldn't go on the way they were. Do you see? It will never be all right that their son didn't have his life. But must his parents suffer forever without any hope?"

Well, that's us, I thought. The no-hope trio. "But it's like they're going ahead and doing something without him. Something he's not part of. It doesn't sound right to me."

"If you saw them, saw the look on their faces, you might not say so," Dad answered.

"It seems so … selfish."

Dad went to stand by the window over the sink, talking to me but facing out toward the backyard. "You know how it feels some mornings like you can't get out of bed? That you wish you didn't have to, it's just too hard to face another day? But you do get up. I get up because of you and Mom, and Mom gets up because of me and you, and you get up because of me and Mom. Because as bad as we feel about living, we know how wrong it would be, how impossible it would be for the others, if something happened to us. So Grace and Frank have been getting up for each other every day, forcing themselves out of bed every day for four years. And now they think they found a better reason to be doing this. To give another child life and happiness. And by doing it, of course, they help themselves. Now they can look forward to the day, to their lives. Do we owe the dead our own lives?" He stopped and turned, looking around the room like he was trying to find the answer. "I don't know. Maybe. Or maybe it's all right to move on." I thought he might cry.

I had quieted down a little. "Do you think they'll keep thinking about their son? And tell the baby about him?"

"Of course. No question."

"Their boy died of cancer?"

"Yeah. Brain tumor. Terrible. Poor thing. All of six years old. Now they'll have a baby. A girl."

"How can they know that—that it's a girl?"

That's when Dad explained about amnio-something and sonograms and stuff like that for checking to see if a baby's okay before it's born. It just made everything seem even stranger.

I felt kind of mixed up, but I told Dad that I'd come along with them if he could persuade Mom to go out. Even to the museum, although who the hell Rauschenberg is I still don't know.

"That'd be great. We could eat out afterward. You know that place you boys, uh, you, like so much. With the smoothies?"

"Yeah. Emerald Planet." Isaac always got the pineapple coconut. And we would sit at the table and play Geography. "Remember how Isaac always wanted to play that dumb game whenever we went to a restaurant? Even though he always lost?"

"Because he was too young to know a lot of places."

"He was starting to learn, wasn't he?"

"Yeah. I guess he was."

"It's so wrong that we'll never know how he would have turned out."

"He would have turned out great." And then Dad really was crying, hard, and didn't bother to hide it.

We never did go anywhere. Dad waved me off, and I went back downstairs. Sam was still playing Zelda. It was one of those I-could-see-he-could-see-I-was-upset moments, but we both decided to pretend nothing was the matter.

8

LADYBUG, LADYBUG

That Monday, for the first time in a long time, I felt like stopping off at Mom's school after my classes were over. It was always kind of fun—playing Battleship or Mousetrap and letting the kids win, or being "it" for a game of Red Light/Green Light. But I stopped going after Isaac. I mean, I never understood how Mom went back to work so soon. Seeing all those other kids. Didn't it make her crazy?

I always thought it was pretty great, though, what she'd made of the place, starting from just a day care center with a handful of kids in the basement of a church. The Saturn School—named after our family. Dad did an amazing job fixing it up. My favorite thing is still the solar system he painted on the ceiling of the hallway, even though it's kind of a cheesy joke about our bizarro last name. Whenever I look up at it, I get a peaceful feeling, like, for a second, I found my place in the universe.

I got there just as the army of after-school kids was straggling in, looking like the survivors of a day on the battlefield. Exhausted. Dragging around those heavy backpacks. Each one seemed to need a Band-Aid or a tissue or juice or a cracker at the exact same moment. No matter how good the teachers are they are always outnumbered. And, man, can little kids talk! It's so funny the way they tell stories—going on and on with every detail they can think of about a trip to the supermarket or some such, mentioning names of people you don't know, like their cousins from Jersey, and then winding up not saying anything that makes much sense.

When they saw me, a couple of the kids started calling my name. It felt good that they remembered me. I went over to one of the little girls.

"Hey, Nikki. Sup?"

She just threw herself into my arms. I could smell the peanut butter on her breath.

"Sit with me, Aaron!"

"Sure. No problemo." I saw Mom smile at me from the back of the room. I hunkered down next to Nikki at the art table, feeling ridiculous in the tiny chair. Colored glue, feathers, stickers, beads, fabric, and buttons were spread out in front of us for collages. I looked around at the other kids at the table and realized it was all girls. A bunch of the boys were busy making a block city and then knocking it down. They hadn't heard that art was cool. I learned that from Lil and Isaac.

Elspeth, one of Mom's teachers, walked around the table, helping kids. We were all working away when I noticed one of the girls kept peeking at something under a pile of construction paper. "Whatcha got there, Hallie?" I asked.

She jerked her head up but didn't say a word. I had scared her. Nikki reached over and lifted up Hallie's paper. "It's stickers!" she cried out, like old Hallie'd been hiding drugs or something. "Hallie's got her own stickers! It's not allowed!"

Hallie narrowed her eyes and shot out a death ray at Nikki. "I was going to share, Nikki," she said. She had that tone like how could anyone doubt she was the world's nicest person. She flashed a great big phony smile to the whole table, showed them the stickers, and then said, like she intended this all along, "Who wants one?" I had to admire how the kid finessed the situation.

The girls all raised their hands and began to shout: "I want one!" "I want a butterfly!"

Sticker Girl wasn't having it. "You can't pick," she told them. "I'm giving them out."

Elspeth rolled her eyes at me and told Hallie to hurry up. Hallie handed the first girl a bumblebee, clearly the loser bug of the lot. But when the girl didn't want it, Hallie let her take a butterfly.

This caused a near-riot. "You let her choose her sticker," some of the girls cried. "That's not fair!"

The whole time Nikki, my pal, kept on drawing with her right hand while she had her left up hand in the air, letting people know she was still in the game to get a sticker but was not about to lower herself by yelling. These kids are Hi-sterical.

Hallie had to give in to popular opinion. "Well, okay. You can choose. But only one each."

The girls crowded around, telling each other which ones they liked and very carefully making their choices. One turned to me and asked, "Which is your favorite, Aaron?"

There was this kid, Justin, maybe eight years old, standing nearby. When he heard that, he made a face like he'd never heard anything so disgusting in his whole life. "Those things are for girls!"

Well, I've never been a big fan of stickers, but I had to take a stand. "Hey, dude," I said to him, "these things are mad pretty!"

He couldn't believe his ears. I bent down next to Hallie and looked over her selection. All the girls were staring at me, just dying to hear what I'd say.

"I have to go with the ladybug."

Justin was horrified. "Aa-ron's a gi-rl," he started to chant.

Elspeth said his name in that flat way teachers have, and he zipped it.

I guess little boys need to go through that macho phase. I know I did. And I remember Isaac, maybe around kindergarten, wearing a towel tied around his neck like it was a superhero cape.

Anyway, after that, all the girls wanted ladybugs, and Hallie ran out. Nikki had to settle for a dragonfly.

9

AN OFF DAY

It was the first game of the season, and just as I was pulling on my green and white socks, Mom let me know she wasn't coming. I was beyond pissed. It makes no sense to me now that I got so mad at her. But I guess I was hurt and thinking: *She was the one who kept pushing me to go back—and now she can't bother showing up?*

Mom said something like, "I didn't think you'd mind, honey. I told An Rui I'd help her at the flea market today. She's teaching me Chinese in exchange!"

"Who? What are you talking about?"

"The woman in the schoolyard the other day."

I went into high sarcastic mode. "Uh ... learning Chinese is more important than coming to my game?"

"Aaron! I never said it's more important."

I was on a roll. "No. You're just doing that instead of watching me play." I concentrated on lacing up my cleats.

"I really didn't think it was such a big deal to you."

"Fine. It's not. What I do is no big deal."

Dad, coming down the stairs, had overheard our conversation. "You know your mother isn't saying that," he told me.

I ignored him, kept going after Mom. "And why in the world do you want to learn Chinese?" I asked, standing up and facing her.

"Why not?"

"That's no answer!"

"Well, maybe not. But I don't like the way you're speaking to me."

I mumbled, "Whatever."

"Look, I'm sorry that I didn't check with you first."

I couldn't let it drop. I just yelled something really mature like, "Forget about it. It's stupid. It doesn't matter." I stormed out of the house with Dad right behind me, telling me I was overreacting, that didn't I know I was the most important thing in her life?

I stopped and answered, "I guess we've just seen the proof of that."

"Would you just cool off and think about it for a second? What it would mean for your mom to be at the game? I can help coach, warm up the batters, talk sports with the other fathers. But Mom has to make small talk with all these women feeling sorry for her. Better to speak in a whole other language with someone she barely knows."

When I look back on that day, I feel like such a dick. I can't believe I said those things to Mom. But I still didn't get why she wanted to learn Chinese. Dad thought it was because it was just something totally different, something that didn't have any connection to anything in her life—or to any bad memories. Sort of like running away in her head.

I told Dad I was sorry. He pointed me back inside, saying, "Tell Mom."

Mom was in my room, sitting on the bed, staring at the floor. When she heard me come in she picked up her head. Before I could open my mouth she started to say that I was right and she should go and all, but I told her it was okay, and I could see she was relieved.

Dad popped his head in and told me get a move on. Mom wished me good luck, and Dad and I hustled up to the park. We were playing the Dragons, who had been in first place for about a million years in a row. I was having some fantasy like it was my time to do something major, hit for the cycle, make some incredible shoestring catch and be like this big hero.

Of course, by the fourth inning, the Gators were getting destroyed. It was five-zip. Not only wasn't I hitting, I had whiffed and grounded out to the pitcher. The outfield was blowing easy pop-ups. And Sean was throwing bricks.

I sat on the bench working myself up into a fit. The way I was thinking then, it seemed to me none of the other guys gave a shit. I made myself really popular when I asked them something along the lines of, "What the hell is wrong with you assholes?"

"Fuck off, Saturn."

I guess I was looking for a fight because I kept going. I called to Sean, "Hey, you're throwing some great batting practice up there. Just one thing: the game actually started four innings ago."

"Like you could do any better. I didn't see you hitting anything."

"Yeah, well, at least I got a couple of guys out, which is a lot more than I can say for some people. If you can't be bothered, maybe you should tell Larry and let somebody pitch who knows how."

"*Fuck you!*" He screamed then jumped up and took a swing at me.

I ducked. "*Ooh.* Was it something I said?"

I dodged another punch but fell back against some of the guys. They pushed me right back toward Sean. I managed to land a blow. Larry came running over and pulled us apart.

"*What the hell is going on here?* You are both out of the game! Do you hear me?"

I was pissed. "Me? *I'm* out of the game? He's losing the game for us and then he hits me and *I'm* out of the game?"

Sean called me a goddamn liar. Larry yelled at us not to say another word. I don't think I'd ever seen Larry that furious. "The two of you. Apologize. Now," he ordered.

"The hell I will," Sean said.

"Then you'll be out next game too."

Larry moved closer until he was practically standing on top of me. "Aaron?"

I didn't answer.

"Aaron!"

I can't believe what came out of my mouth then. I looked up at Larry, then over to Sean. "I'm sorry. I'm sorry you're such a shitty pitcher."

Some of the guys were laughing, but Larry was beyond angry.

"You just came back. You want to be out the whole season?"

Someone shouted out, "Suck it up, Saturn."

The look in Larry's eyes made me realize he wasn't kidding. "I'm sorry I got after you," I told Sean. "I'm sorry I hit you."

"Yeah. Me too," Sean mumbled.

I sat down and looked over to where Dad was standing. I'd always heard people talk about the look of a deer caught in the headlights. Like you were so stunned you couldn't figure out what the hell was up. Well, that's what Dad looked like that day.

But it was a weird thing. After the fight, the team started to play better. We began to catch up. It was hard just to be on the bench and watch. We actually wound up winning.

When we were packing up, Larry pulled me aside.

"Look, I know that wasn't like you. I've never seen you blow up before—actually throw a punch. You have to keep it under control. You can't go beating up on my pitcher."

By then I was feeling like a total schmuck. And I meant it when I said, "I know. I'm sorry."

"Just don't let it happen again." Larry gave me a small smile. "Even when he's having an off day."

"Sure, Coach."

"See you at practice."

"Right."

Before he came over to me, Dad spoke for a minute to Larry and to Sean and his father. Then he asked if I was okay.

"Yeah. I guess."

"Maybe it wasn't such a great idea, your coming back. Maybe it's too soon."

Well, I could see how he came to that conclusion. But I realized I had had a good time—even with the stupid fight. I wanted to keep playing ball. I told him that.

"All right, then. I like watching you play. Except for the part when you're whaling on people."

I told him I didn't know what got into me. But I guess we both knew. He put his arm around my shoulder, and we walked home together through the now-green park.

10

LITTLE BUDDHA

When I got back to my room I noticed there was a small statue of a smiling man sitting on my dresser. I still keep it there. It looks like a piece of driftwood, sort of like what we used to find on the beach in Maine. The swirls in the wood form the folds of his robe. It feels good—smooth and cool when I run my fingers over it. When I first saw him, I thought about the Chinese art book in the store on St. Mark's Place, those funny little men. I realized Mom probably had gotten it for me from the Chinese lady.

I went upstairs holding the statue to find Mom. She was in the kitchen, looking through the pantry and refrigerator, making up a shopping list. I asked her if the little guy was from her. She nodded and said that she was worried I wouldn't like it, but I told her I liked it a lot. Then she explained that it was a Buddha or some Chinese god. "There are so many of them. An Rui wasn't entirely sure."

"Well, whoever it is, I think it's great."

"I'm glad. Consider it a peace offering."

"Sorry."

"I am too."

She took the figure from my hand. "I was just drawn to it. It was like you somehow."

"A fat little wooden man?"

She laughed. "No. The face coming out of the wood. You can make it out, but not quite completely. And that it's smiling. A good person."

Right, I thought. "If I was, maybe I would have done something for Isaac."

Mom took a breath. "Honey, we've been over and over this."

"But …"

"There's no 'but,'" she said, looking hard at me. "Don't you think I'm always asking myself if I missed something? If there was something, anything, I could have done? I don't want you to keep torturing yourself about it. I have to believe if there was the least sign, the smallest indication of a problem, we all would have done whatever we could."

"I know, Mom. I know."

She didn't say anything for a minute. Then she asked me, "Did something happen at the game today?"

"Yeah. And you might want to take back that good person rating. Dad didn't tell you?"

"He just mentioned something about a misunderstanding."

"Yeah. I misunderstood how not to be an idiot, ragged on Sean and actually hit him. Larry was really pissed."

She was pretty surprised. Dad obviously had not provided details. "Why would you hit him? Why did Sean get you so angry?"

I gave her a brief version, emphasizing how sorry I was. She just listened and didn't ask me anything else, except, when I finished, if I had plans for the rest of the day because she and Dad were supposed to go out with the Millers.

"The Millers? Uh, the ones who are going to have, like, a baby?"

"The very ones."

I wasn't sure I should say anything, but I asked her, "Are you unhappy about that?"

She looked down at the statue. "I'm trying very hard not to be." Then she said with a sharp little laugh, "Not that it's working."

I waited for her to get her thoughts together.

"I'm not sure this makes sense, but I feel I've kind of lost them in a way because they have a new focus. And I'm jealous they have that. I resent it. And I don't like that I'm turning into a bitter person."

"Why not? Why shouldn't we be bitter?"

"Oh, honey, there's a difference between being angry, being hurt, and turning everything into something ugly." She kept talking, trying to control her voice. She hesitated each time before saying Isaac's name. "You know, before … we … lost … Isaac, I guess I just took for granted that I knew how to be a mother, a teacher, that I was doing fine. But now I question everything. What's the best way to live my life now? What's the right thing for you? I'm sorry if Dad and I don't always know what to do for you. Like about baseball. You know we're trying to find our way through this."

I nodded. I didn't know what to say except to thank her for the statue.

She kissed me and handed the little Buddha back. I went down to my room and lay down on my bed, still holding it. I thought it was so eerie—almost like Mom knew I had seen that Chinese art book. Almost like she knew I was thinking of her then. I looked at the statue, but I didn't see the resemblance between it and me. I still don't. Except for the not being completely formed part. Sometimes I think the only thing that's complete about me is my stupidity.

You know who the statue really reminds me of? Isaac. Because he never had the chance to become his whole self. Maybe it's both of us. It doesn't really matter. Mom felt some connection to it, and so do I. I still like looking at it. It calms me down.

That day it calmed me so much I fell fast asleep.

When I woke up, Dad was sitting on my bed. He told me I'd been sleeping for a couple of hours.

"I guess I was exhausted. I'm just not used to all the exercise."

"I guess."

I apologized again for what had happened at the game. Dad brushed it off like it was nothing epic. It's good to have parents who don't need to beat on you when you're already beating up on yourself.

To tell the truth, we were both thinking more about the baby thing than my acting like a dick at the game.

"Dad? Could you, you guys … I mean … a baby? Is that something that could happen?"

Dad looked down and started to run his hand back and forth along the bedspread.

"Well, we're a little old for that, A-Team. It wouldn't be totally impossible, but it sure wouldn't be easy."

"You guys aren't so old. I guess. I think. Not that I know much about it."

"Thanks, kiddo, but we are, for any number of reasons. You're asking this because of Frank and Grace, right? The Millers?"

"Yeah."

"Look. I'll be honest. When they told us, well, the thought flashed through my mind. Your mother's too, of course. We talked about it some. And for a moment, well, imagining a baby—it was so … sweet. But then we considered our age and what might go wrong and we dropped the idea."

"What could go wrong?"

"You remember when I told you about amnio?"

"Sort of."

Then Dad started to explain almost like he was giving a lesson in front of a class. I could tell he had been reading up on it. It sounded pretty grim—miscarriage, stillbirth, Down syndrome. And you can find out with the tests they have, before the baby is born, if there's something wrong. I asked him what happened then.

"Well, you could decide to end the pregnancy."

"You're talking about abortion, right?"

"Right. And we couldn't imagine doing that. Not after …"

It was a lot to deal with. First thinking about a new baby. Then thinking about a sick baby. Or a nonbaby.

Dad stood up quickly, like he wanted to wrap up the conversation. "Let's just say that babies, any baby, take a lot of effort, a lot of time. Mom and I are not sure we have that in us anymore. So that's that."

But there was something in his voice that sounded like what he was saying wasn't really what was in his heart. Which meant maybe he wanted a baby. Which meant Mom might too. Probably even more. But it seemed like they weren't going to do it. Which would make them sadder. And, instead of caring, I was relieved. Which made me feel like shit.

11

SPRING AND FALL

I started going once or twice a week to the Saturn School. It took up the afternoons when I had no practice or Sam was too busy to hang. One rainy day late in spring the kids were going a bit nutso being cooped up inside. In bad weather the place could get kind of gloomy: because it was in the basement, it wasn't exactly flooded with light even when the sun was out. Elspeth asked me to get Mom, who was in her office. "Tell her I need help! The kids are about to paint me."

I was glad to have an excuse to leave the classroom for a minute. I walked down the hall toward Mom's office. When I got near the door I heard someone talking to her.

"Look, Claire," a man was saying, "I am really sorry about what happened. A terrible tragedy. And you've been very brave to come back and shoulder your responsibilities. Don't think I'm not sensitive to that. But I have to think of my own child. I don't think it's right to have Hallie exposed to it. I've wanted to move her for a long time, but there was no place that had an opening. But now I'm going to pull her out. Four is too young to have to hear about death."

What a schmuck, talking to Mom that way! I wanted to bust in and pound him.

Mom was speaking softly. I could barely hear her over my breathing. She said something about what had happened back on 9/11 and how the school was a safe place to talk about things like that, or about pets or grandparents checking out.

"You give them fears when you talk about it."

This guy was an asshole! I was epically angry. I don't think I got that way a lot before Isaac died. Then all this started to come up from inside me.

Mom was quiet for a minute. She was probably trying to control her voice. Then she began talking about Isaac. And how the kids had seen her so upset and she couldn't lie to them. Then about why it was a bad idea to be pulling out his kid—Hallie the Drama Queen—so suddenly.

The man blah-blahed on and I didn't know how Mom could stand it. I had an image of him as some Wall Street type in a suit, but when he finally stepped out of the room I saw he was wearing paint-splattered jeans and a T-shirt. I stared at his back and fantasized jumping him or something, totally forgetting about the fight I'd just been in.

I walked into the office. Mom was looking out the window, watching the rain fall in the empty play yard.

I told her I'd heard the guy. "What a putz."

"People sometimes act impulsively. Or from the wrong motives. And they think they're being reasonable."

"People are stupid."

She laughed, but then told me she was worried about Sticker Girl. I was too, having seen her in action.

I said it was so fucked up that this guy should have a kid and maybe ruin her life and we should lose Isaac.

"Children die. Beautiful, wonderful children. It's never fair." She made a strange noise at the back of her throat.

I asked if she was okay. And she said, "Yeah. Never better."

Maybe this is where my sarcastic sense of humor comes from.

I asked if the guy could be right, that talking about death would just scare the kids.

"*Not* talking about it scares them. To see people sad and not be able to ask, to know that someone or something important isn't there anymore but you're not supposed to talk about it, to think that your feelings aren't normal. This guy wants to pretend that people don't die. That children don't die."

We were both quiet for a bit. Then she told me something about myself when I was little. She knows I love hearing stuff like that. She said that when I was about Hallie's age I started to ask about death.

"One night, when I was putting you to bed, you asked what had happened to your grandparents, and I told you they had died. It made you very sad. The next night you asked about me and Dad, would we die too? And I said we would, although not for a long while. You were even sadder. The following night you asked, 'What about my friends? Are they going to die?' And I had to say yes. You were miserable. And then, the night after that, you asked, 'Am *I* going to die?' And when I said you would—even though it would be a long, long time from then, when you were very old—you cried."

"But it doesn't always turn out that way."

"No," she sighed. "No it doesn't."

She put her arms around me and held me for a moment. Then she told me about a sad poem she always thought about by this guy Hopkins: "Spring and Fall: To a Young Child."

We had read some of his stuff in English class, and I hadn't liked it then. This one is about a little girl, Margaret, crying over the falling leaves in autumn:

It is the blight man was born for,
It is Margaret you mourn for.

I looked it up afterwards and memorized the whole thing.

12

MAGICAL THINKING

Maybe because I'd been hanging out at the school and had kids on my mind, I started thinking a lot about Owen, who had his appointment with Dr. Orbach after mine. So at my next session I asked Orbach how the little dude was doing. Being a shrink, he bounced the question right back to me and asked me why I wanted to know. I told him it was because I thought he was not that happy a kid. I said not happy because I didn't think it would be cool to say bizarro.

"In what way does he seem unhappy to you?"

"Come on." He had to be joking.

"No. Tell me what you think."

"Well, he seems alone."

"You feel sorry for him?"

"I guess."

"And what would you like to see happen?"

I hadn't really thought out that part, but when Orbach asked me, I came up with an answer.

"Maybe he should go to my mom's school. For after-school, I mean. He's too old for nursery school."

Orbach seemed surprised. I surprised myself too. I used to want to avoid Owen and there I was suggesting something that would mean I'd see him a few times a week.

"My mom and the other teachers would make sure nobody made fun of him. He'd have a good time there. He looks like he could use a good time."

"Why do you think kids might make fun of him?"

I rolled my eyes. "You know better than anyone. He's a weir—uh, unusual kid."

Orbach didn't say anything for a minute. He did that a lot. If the guy got paid by the word, he'd be broke. I asked him what he thought of my idea.

"I think you're a very thoughtful person. In both senses of the word."

"I don't mean about me! I mean about Owen."

"Yes, I know, Aaron."

Orbach said it wasn't easy to convince people that you know better than they do. I realized Orbach was talking about Owen's mother, but I was thinking about Hallie's father.

I was comparing Mom and Dad to them and was grateful that they were way, way better. But then things began to go off track.

A few days after my talk with Orbach when we were having dinner—actually only pizza—Dad started talking about how he had been at Lil's house and was going to fix it up. Mom stopped eating.

"You never said anything about doing that, Barry."

"Is there a problem?"

"Well, no, but I wish you'd told me."

"I'm telling you now. I just decided."

She sat looking down at her slice for a moment. "I guess it makes sense," she said. "We should have gotten it ready to sell awhile ago. If things had been … different. It's been empty too long."

That's when Dad told us that he didn't think we should sell it.

"What do you mean?" Mom asked. "Didn't you just say you were over there to get it ready to put on the market?"

"I didn't say that."

"Do you mean rent it out? I'm not sure I want to deal with that."

"No. Not rent it. I think we should sell *this* place and move over there."

Mom was so shocked she didn't say anything. And I was confused.

"Dad, isn't that a whole lot of trouble just to go across the street?"

"Yeah. But it's the kind of trouble I like. And it would be a new beginning."

That's when Mom started crying. "Without Isaac, you mean. A new house without our boy."

Dad got up and put his hands on her shoulders. "Claire, we don't have to. I'm sorry, okay?"

"I don't know. I can't imagine—"

"Maybe it'll be good for us. A change."

When Dad said that it made me think that, if we did something like that, made any kind of change, it would mean we accepted Isaac was dead. Was never coming back. You'd think I already knew it. But that night I realized some small part of me had never truly believed he was gone. That if things kept more or less the same … crazy, right? Later I talked about it a lot with Orbach. He said it was magical thinking.

"I don't think it's such a good idea," I said. "Like it'd be weird to move away from where Isaac lived."

"It's just across the street. To Lil's house," Dad said.

"It's still moving!"

"Look, I—"

"And what about Isaac's stuff? All his clothes, his books? His art?"

"We'll take them, of course."

It just seemed so awful, the idea of packing up his life. I was angry at Dad for bringing up the idea. "Why bother?" I asked him, really nasty. "We should just sell his things, like we did with Lil's."

Mom took a sharp breath. "Aaron!"

Dad was furious. "How dare you say that?"

Mom stood up. "I won't listen to this!" she yelled as she ran out of the room.

Dad started to follow her but turned and slumped back in his chair.

Me and Dad sat there, silently blaming each other. I was thinking: *this is what passes for quality time. Mom hysterical, Dad pissed.*

After a minute he pushed away from the table, shaking his head, and began heading upstairs.

"I'm sorry, Dad," I apologized lamely.

"I shouldn't have said anything," he mumbled.

I sat there at the table with the cold pizza. And I remembered the strangest thing. The time when Mom wanted a new dining room table to replace the very one I was sitting at. I guess Isaac was about six or seven. He begged her not to. We thought it was so strange—what could he care about a piece of furniture? But Mom realized it was because he didn't want anything in the house to change. He wouldn't let it drop, and finally she gave in. There I was at that same old table. I had the thought that if he didn't want a new table, he sure as hell wouldn't want a new house! He wouldn't want to move. And if we did—and I know this sounds insane—would he know where we'd gone? How would he be able to find us?

13

BIG-NOSED DUDE

Call me a perv, but even with everything that was going on, I was thinking about girls. Well, *a* girl. I guess no matter what, there's always a part of a guy's brain with sex on it.

I'm not sure when I first noticed Emma. She came to our school a year after I did, in seventh grade, but I was a dumb twelve-year-old, and she wasn't on my radar yet.

I guess I should give myself some credit—after Isaac died, I didn't think about her for a while. But almost as soon as I went back to school I found myself looking at her every chance I got. She's not beautiful or anything, not the way people in the movies are. She's just a tall, thin girl with light brown hair and green eyes. Maybe I don't like her in the usual way guys like girls. Not that I have a clue as to what the usual way of liking a girl is. I just always wanted to see her. We were in two classes together, French and biology. I'd watch her in bio, sitting on a stool at the lab table, leaning over to take notes, every now and then brushing back her hair. There's something quiet about her. At times, I guess when she's thinking about something else, she kind of zones out with a tiny smile on her face. I just love that.

Of course, I'd be staring at her in class, not knowing what was going on, and Dr. Walsh would call on me. He always uses last names, and he liked to pick on me, especially when I wasn't paying attention, so he could make the joke of saying, "Earth to Saturn." The other kids groaned every time he did that, but it never stopped him.

I didn't really mind him ragging on me. At least he didn't think he had to handle me like a special case. I just hoped the whole class didn't notice I was looking at Emma—and prayed she didn't, either. I mean I wanted her to notice, but in a good way—not think I was some kind of creeper.

I knew I couldn't go on acting like such an idiot about her. I didn't know what to do, though. Luckily I had Sam to talk it over with. Not that he was an expert on the subject, but he was what I had. I brought it up one afternoon while we were sitting on my front stoop. It was a warm day, the kind of day that almost felt like summer, and both of us were avoiding going inside and doing homework.

"I feel bad spending time caring about a girl when it hasn't been that long after losing my brother. It's like I'm this selfish schmuck."

Sam said it was okay. "You're being too hard on yourself."

I mean, what else would a best friend say?

"It's normal," he added. "Downright age-appropriate."

"But I feel like there's something wrong with me."

I never should have given Sam an opening like that.

"Oh, well, now," he said, looking me up and down. "I'm not saying there isn't—the list is long and time is short. But liking a girl is not one of the many things wrong with you."

"At this point I haven't even talked to her, except maybe to ask if she was finished using the microscope." I tried to explain what I felt about Emma. "I just want to be near her. Like not even talking. Please don't laugh, but I have this idea that we'd understand each other without words."

Sam made a face. I could see he was forcing himself not to say how dumb I sounded.

"Okay, I know it's cheesy," I said quickly.

Sam shook his head. "Way beyond that." Then he gave me this huge smile. "Actually, it's adorable."

"Thanks a lot. What you mean is I'm a total and complete loser."

"Didn't say it."

"Didn't have to."

"No, seriously, you're a no bigger idiot than any other kid our age."

"Then I'm in trouble."

"You know it," Sam laughed, digging in his backpack for some candy.

"What should I do?"

"Make a move," Sam said, pulling out a smushed chocolate bar.

"Like what? Like tell her I think she's hot?" I asked sarcastically.

"Maybe not. That might not be the best approach, rap notwithstanding."

"Ask her out on a date?"

"Too retro."

"Well, what then?"

"It doesn't have to be a date. You just conspire to chill. Come up with a specific chilling opportunity."

"How do I do that?"

Sam looked up at the sky as if he wanted to make sure God was catching this. "He's fourteen years old. And I have to explain to him how to chill."

"Very funny."

He took a bite of the chocolate bar and offered the brown lump to me.

I waved it away. "No, thank you—but hey, thanks for the thought."

"I'm a little gentleman," Sam said, finishing off the chocolate and licking his fingers. "So? Any ideas rattling around?"

I admitted to him that because I had found out what Emma's last class was, most days I saw her leaving school. And I knew which way she walked. It made me sound like a stalker.

"Uh. Am I missing something here? You've got everything in place. Why don't you just go up and talk to her?"

"I guess I could do that. If I was a different person. Someone who wasn't afraid he'd say something really stupid and spit all over her while he was at it."

"I think I'm beginning to see the dimensions of the dilemma," Sam said, rolling his eyes. He clapped me on the shoulder with his smeared fingers. "But I have faith in you, boy. You can do it."

"But I don't have a clue what to say to her."

"Details, details. Talk about homework or movies or something. The weather's a classic, if oft-mocked, topic."

"Global warming?"

"There you go. Talk about the plight of the polar bears. I mean, you know, not only are those poor suckers floating around on tinier and tinier chunks of ice, they're shrinking. Losing the pounds."

I wasn't sure how we got on the subject of polar bears, but that's Sam for you. I thought about how dumb I would sound going up to Emma and, out of nowhere, suddenly asking, "So what do you think about the polar bear situation?" When I stopped laughing, I asked Sam if he would help me.

"Help you talk to her?"

"Well, yeah."

"Like Cyrano?"

"What the hell is that?"

"Oh, please. You, my well-read friend, don't know the Cyrano story? What kind of world is this where teenagers are not familiar with nineteenth-century French literature?"

I stared at him. "Who *are* you?"

"Just listen up. There was this dude with a big nose and he writes love notes for this other handsome dude so he—handsome dude—can get this girl. The girl goes crazy for the notes and she thinks she loves the handsome dude because she thinks he wrote them. But she doesn't realize it's the big-nosed dude who wrote the letters and that he loves her and she really loves him. Until the end, of course, when somebody dies and it's too late."

For some reason that just seemed HI-sterical. Better even than the incredible shrinking polar bears. "Big-nosed dude?"

"They made a movie out of it. Several actually."

"They made a movie about a guy with a big nose?"

"You're missing the point here, bro. If I talk for you, the fair Emma will fall in love with *me.* "

I think Sam is funny as hell, but maybe funny isn't what girls are looking for. Not in a boyfriend, anyway.

I thought of the time in seventh grade I had tried to help him out with this girl, Alexis, he'd had a crush on.

"Hey. You owe me. Remember Alexis?" I asked him. "How I had to walk with you past her house for weeks in case we ran into her?"

Sam put his hands over his ears. "I can't hear you," he chanted. Then he got up and starting running up the block like a madman. A woman was walking in the opposite direction pushing a stroller. She steered well away from him.

I yelled at him to come back. The woman looked at both of us like we were a pair of dangerous dope fiends.

Sam plopped back down next to me. "Ah, Alexis. My favorite part was when she told me about how much she liked some other guy." He made a face. "I'm fated to be 'liked as a friend' forever."

I shook my head. "Give it time."

Sam smiled. "But you're moment is now. Seize the day. *Carpe* the ol' *diem* as the saying goes."

"I'm not sure I'm ready for this, to go to the front lines."

"Many brave men have been lost in the cause before us," Sam said, standing up again and saluting me. He grabbed his backpack. "Well, time to hit the books, or cook the books, or burn the books, whichever comes first. I'm so glad we had this little chat. Let me know what happens."

"Hey, where are you going? You haven't said if you'll help me!"

"You can do this, soldier," Sam said, hoisting up his pack.

By now I was begging. "Come with me tomorrow. Talk to her."

"I warned you. I'll steal her from you with my wit and charm," Sam said over his shoulder as he went down the stairs.

"Right. Meet me tomorrow?"

He kept walking, but I could hear him say, "Yeah, yeah."

"Thanks," I yelled.

"What would you do without me?" he shouted back.

I watched him as he made his way up the block. And I said very softly, "I really don't know."

14

DADDY'S LITTLE GIRL

When Operation Talk to a Girl Day came, I was frantic. I couldn't concentrate on anything; it was like I had dreamed going to my classes. My last subject was Phys Ed. I was taking fencing. There I was in those ridiculous padded clothes, getting pinged by the other kid the whole hour because I wasn't paying attention to what the hell I was doing. Every time his foil touched me the damn electronic beeper would go off. It was like being inside Smash Brothers.

I hadn't planned well because I was pretty sweaty after that. I walked up and down Pierrepont Street hoping to dry off. Of course, I was so nervous I just sweated more. I was trying to see in two directions at once—looking for Sam in front of me coming from Clinton Street and Emma behind me leaving school. I spotted Emma first, walking with her usual crew, Meredith and Olivia, who I sort of knew from class. I started nodding and grinning at them like I was some kind of bobblehead. I was praying for Sam to show. The girls seemed to be having some sort of discussion. And then, totally unexpectedly, Olivia called out to me that they were going for pizza, did I want to come? I was so surprised I muttered something snappy like, "I'm waiting for someone."

"That's cool," Olivia said. "We'll be at Happy's. You and your friend should come."

I walked over to them and, like a real idiot, said, "The pizza's pretty bad there."

Meredith rolled her eyes. "Du-uh. But it's the closest."

Just then I noticed Sam, in pink pants and a yellow shirt, come up the block. I guess everyone else in Brooklyn did too. He stopped in front of us.

"Your friend?" Olivia asked.

I nodded.

"It figures."

Sam gave her a huge smile. "I am Sam. Sam I am." He made a bow.

I was so jumpy I didn't say anything. Sam told them he was "delighted to meet such beautiful ladies."

We all walked over to Court Street, Sam doing most of the talking. As I recall, he, Meredith, and Olivia were arguing over who went to a tougher school. Once Sam told them he had to take Latin, they conceded.

Emma didn't say one word to me the whole way. I was really uncomfortable. Then, when we were at the counter placing our order, I realized that I was actually going to have to eat in front of her. As if I didn't feel awkward enough. I was afraid I would drip sauce all over my shirt. So I just asked for a soda. Yeah, I was a coward. Sam gave me a look and ordered two slices with extra cheese just to show me up.

We managed to get a booth, but it was really only big enough for four. Sam dragged over a stool and balanced on top of it. He looked like a crane or some other kind of hunched-over bird with long legs. Emma asked if he was okay.

Sam told her, "I'm good," and then twisted himself into some sort of pretzel. "This is where the yoga comes in handy."

Olivia glanced at him and narrowed her eyes. "Half Lord of the Fishes?"

"That's me."

I sat sipping my drink, desperate for something to say, trying not to stare too much at Emma. Even in the greenish light of the pizzeria she looked good. Luckily, the girls were jabbering away. I gathered from the conversation that Emma's fifteenth birthday was coming up the next week. Meredith was giving her a hard time for not having a party.

Emma asked, "Why should every year be this pretend-important occasion?"

That got everyone else talking about Bar and Bat Mitzvahs at thirteen and Sweet Sixteens and the drinking and voting ages. I was glad for all the noise because it covered up the rumbling of my empty stomach. Then Sam mentioned something called a *quinceañera*. None of us had ever heard of it.

"They're these outrageous parties Latino parents throw their daughters at fifteen. Sometimes they're like mini-weddings," he explained. "The girls wear crazy fancy dresses, and their fathers actually give them crowns and stuff."

Meredith asked how he knew about it.

"All cultures are open to me," he told her in his phony-grand manner. "I'm a student of the world." At that moment, about to fall off his stool, he looked more like an actual idiot.

"Crowns? Right," Emma said, shaking her head. "I can just see my father treating me like I was a princess."

"Maybe Her Royal Highness of You Are Not Allowed to Stop Taking Flute Lessons," Olivia remarked.

"Or My Lady of You Have to Go to Soccer Practice," Emma added. "Duchess of Don't Embarrass Me at the Dance Recital."

"He's pretty much a hardass?" I asked.

"Let's just say that whole Daddy's Little Girl thing is lost on him."

She sounded kind of angry. It was the first time I thought about her as a person with problems of her own. From what she was saying, I figured maybe it wasn't so much that she didn't want a party but that her parents, or at least her dad, wouldn't let her have one, so she was pretending she didn't care.

Meredith asked, "How do people decide what special ages to make a major thing out of, anyway?"

"Yeah," Olivia agreed. "Like, why Sweet Sixteen?"

Emma laughed. "I think we all know one or two sixteen-year-olds. We might call them many things, but sweet isn't one of them."

I nodded. "How about Half-Sour Sixteen?"

"Sea Salt Sixteen?" Emma suggested.

Sam wiggled his eyebrows. "Hot-and-Spicy Sixteen?"

"Whatever we call it, I guess it's supposed to mean that a girl isn't a child anymore. Her birthday comes around—*poof*—she's magically grown up," Meredith said.

"And boys don't have Sweet Sixteens because they never grow up!" Olivia added.

I smiled. "I won't take that personally."

"Nor I," Sam added. "I believe I'm in synch with the Japanese system. There's something called 'Adult Day' for twenty-year-olds."

"Thank you, Mr. Wikipedia," I said. Only Sam knows stuff like that. People always tell me I'm smart, but I'm not Sam-smart.

"Thirteen, fifteen, sixteen, twenty," Emma repeated. "It's just so arbitrary."

"Whatever," Meredith shrugged. "Any excuse for a party." She gave Emma a meaningful look.

Emma stuck her tongue out at her. "It's stupid. Why should I give myself a party for just living another year?"

"That's right," Sam agreed. "Your friends should give you a party!"

Olivia aimed a balled-up napkin at him. Everyone but me laughed because I couldn't shake off Emma's remark about living another year. I guess I looked pretty upset because suddenly everyone realized how I might take what Emma had said, and they all started to apologize.

"I'm sorry, Aaron," Emma said. "We shouldn't be joking like that."

Just what I didn't want—Emma feeling sorry for me.

"It's fine. I mean, I hate it when everyone has to worry about every little thing they say to me. I've had enough of it."

"I didn't mean to be hurtful. It's just hard to figure out what's okay and what's not."

"That's the point. I don't want people to always be thinking about my feelings. It's pathetic."

I was torn. I liked that she gave a shit, but felt like a stray animal she was petting. Like one of Crazy Harold's loser dogs. And that ain't sexy.

Sam, Buddha be praised, stepped in. "I say we're young, we're thoughtless. We should live in the moment. So how's about a round of Italian ices? On me!"

They all got distracted talking about rainbow versus chocolate. Of course, Olivia had to let us know how disgusting and inorganic all the flavors were.

Everyone else was kidding around again. But not me. I couldn't shake the idea of all those years of life, just regular, stupid life, Isaac would never have. And I started to feel kind of bad for myself too. That things would never be easy again. That I was never again going to be, like Sam had just said, young and thoughtless.

To keep myself from crying, I stared at Sam and the occasional bit of cherry ice that dropped from the soggy paper cup down his hand and onto his pants. I was thinking that being alive did deserve a party.

At least that.

15

KAN KAN YI XIA

I wanted to do something for Emma because her father was messing up her birthday. So I decided to buy her a present, without having any idea what I should give her. I couldn't think of how to go about getting something except to ask Mom. She had forgiven me for my crack about selling Isaac's stuff, and none of us had mentioned the move again.

I didn't want Mom to get the wrong idea, like I had a girlfriend or anything, but I needed advice. Mom was really happy I was talking about something normal. Of course, she asked me all sorts of questions like what's her name and did she know her and where did she live and who were her parents and what did she look like.

"It's just this girl," I told her. "No big deal."

"Just a girl you want to buy a present for. Something you've never done before. Nothing special." She made her eyes wide and tried not to smile. "Got it." Oh, yeah, she believed me.

"Mo-om!"

"Okay, okay. Let me think."

First she suggested that I make Emma something. "People always like handmade gifts."

I shot that down pretty quickly. "What, like the kids in your school do? I'm not four years old." Then I added, even meaner, "And I'm not the artistic one."

That really bothered her. "Look, do you want me to help you or not?"

"I'm sorry. Really."

Mom nodded and made some more suggestions, but we had a hard time coming up with something.

"Girls like clothes, right?" I asked her.

"Do you know her size?"

"Oh, man, this is getting way too complicated. Does it matter?"

"Does it matter?" she laughed. "What if it doesn't fit? What would she do with it? And if you get her something too big she'll be insulted. How about jewelry?"

"That's way too boyfriend–girlfriend."

"A book?"

"I don't know what she likes to read. Or *if* she likes to read."

Mom shook her head. "Why don't we just go out and look?"

So we wound up doing something I never thought I'd do—shopping. I mean, sometimes I help with buying stuff at the supermarket or bodega or hardware store. I buy school supplies. I've even bought myself a pair of jeans. But this was different.

There were all these clothing stores in the neighborhood I never knew about before. I mean, I'd seen them from the outside but had no idea what went on inside, what strange girl-things took place. Secret rituals performed in the dressing rooms. Sacrifices to the gods of fashion. I was weirded out by the whole idea. And going around with my mother on top of that? Mom thought it was pretty funny how I was stressing.

She took me to place after place with short, punchy names like Kiwi, Loom, and Bird, where I couldn't believe how much things cost. It must be some sort of rule—the shorter the name the higher the price. Then we walked a few blocks further away to another part of the neighborhood, and it was suddenly like a whole other world—a world of 99-cent schlock shops and Payless, and jewelry stores you need to be buzzed into where the clerks sit behind bulletproof glass.

We spent most of an afternoon trooping in and out of stores and getting nothing until we were both wiped. But just before we went home Mom asked if I'd mind checking out An Rui's table at the flea market in the schoolyard. That was Mom's Chinese friend. The first one. I wasn't so sure about it. I mean, I liked the Buddha and all, but I still thought it kind of strange that Mom was hanging out with this Chinese lady so much. Not that Mom and Dad were ever prejudiced or snobs or like that, but they had standard-issue friends. White, middle-class, with one or two kids. I don't know if they ever had a Black or Latino or Asian friend. Lil's friends had been more ... unusual. But Mom was changing.

I figured I had nothing to lose, so I agreed to go see An Rui. Mom led me past the clothes and rugs and paintings hanging on the iron fence surrounding the yard and then around the crowd of tables that were heaped with dishes, toys, medals, and old magazines. It was like going through a maze. An Rui was all the way in the rear, set up against the first-floor windows of the school. She and Mom started talking back and forth in Chinese. I realized that Mom had learned a lot.

"*Ni hao ma,*" An Rui said.

"*Wo hen hao, xie xie. Ni ne?*"

"*Wo ye hen hao.*"

Mom pointed to me. "*Zhe shi wo de da er zi.*"

"Ah, Aaron! Hello!" An Rui spoke with a heavy accent.

I nodded at her. "Hi."

"*Ta yao mai yi ge li wu gei ta de nu peng you,*" Mom said.

I couldn't follow what Mom was saying, but, from the way An Rui was smiling, I guessed Mom was telling her I had a girlfriend. I was embarrassed, and also pissed that Mom was telling this stranger stuff about me.

An Rui motioned toward the things she had on display. "Look. *Kan kan yi xia.*"

I could feel that I'd turned bright red. I bent my head down to try to hide it and glanced at what was there—piles of what looked like coral branches, carved wood boxes in different shapes, little metal horses, necklaces made out of green or purple stones. Standing in a row were a few small glass bottles with stoppers in them and pictures painted on the sides. I picked one up. On one side of it was a long-legged bird flying over a lake. It reminded me of Sam. On the other was a house in the middle of some trees. A woman was standing on a balcony, looking out toward a mountain. There was something about it I really liked.

"Uh, how much is this?" I asked.

"Ah. Very nice," An Rui answered. "Painting inside bottle. Twenty dollars."

Mom jumped right in. "*Shi wu kuai? Hao ba?*" I guessed she was bargaining. That made me even more uncomfortable.

"*Shi ba kuai,*" An Rui said.

Mom didn't give up. "*Shi liu kuai, hao bu hao?*"

An Rui nodded. "*Hao.*"

Mom told me it was sixteen bucks. I counted out the money and handed it to An Rui. She poked her head under the table and came back up with a blue and white cloth box to fit the bottle. She put Emma's present inside and gave it to me.

"*Xie xie,*" Mom said. She looked almost happy. And I remember being surprised that this little thing, finding a present, would bring a moment of happiness.

I told Mom I was pretty impressed with all the Chinese she seemed to know. "You can really say something! Not just count to ten or whatever."

"Oh, it's nothing, really. Just very basic stuff. But it helps fill my brain up with something, you know?"

"Yeah, I do."

We walked back home together without speaking, but with the same thought in our heads. Isaac wasn't there anymore, but he was always with us.

16

GIRLS ARE PEOPLE TOO

What I hadn't considered was that, as awkward as it had been, shopping was actually the easy part. I needed to *give* Emma the present. I hadn't exactly thought through that end of it. I began to sweat it—what if she didn't want it? What if she thought it was stupid? What if she thought *I* was stupid? I felt totally pathetic. But I knew that if I didn't give her the gift I'd feel even worse—a complete loser.

I brought it to school that Monday in my backpack. All morning I was totally fixated on it, like I was expecting it to start glowing like a radioactive substance or beeping or even explode, taking out half the school.

Just before lunch Emma and I had French together, so I decided that was when I should make my move. I walked into the room and managed to make it over to her desk without tripping. I sort of shoved the box in her face, mumbling something like, "Here. This is for you. Happy birthday."

She blinked hard. "Wow. Thanks. I can't believe you remembered it was my birthday." She looked like she was blushing, which made me feel a little better. One of those "girls are people too" moments.

"NBD," I shrugged, then, proud of my cleverness, added, *"Bonne anniversaire."*

"Should I open it now?"

Suddenly I was aware of the rest of the class staring at us. Could I have been dumber, giving her the present in front of everyone?

Emma realized at the same moment that we were the center of attention, and stuffed the box into her bag. "Maybe later would be better."

"Good thinking. After class?"

"Lunch?"

I nodded, and couldn't prevent myself from grinning like a fool. I went back to my seat and tried to pretend nothing had happened, but the whole period all I could do was stare at Emma's back, totally oblivious to what else was going on.

Of course, Madame Stossman called me out. *"Monsieur Saturn. Tu n'écoutes pas!"* But I didn't care. *C'est la vie.*

After class Emma left the room first and waited for me in the hallway. We started walking toward the front door. I had to tell myself to keep breathing. Once outside, I had no idea which direction to turn in, where we should go. I had some vague notion that the guy was supposed to be in charge. Probably from the old black-and-white movies I sometimes watched with Mom and Dad. The whole opening the door and helping on with the coat thing. But, clueless, I asked Emma what she wanted to do.

"Well, if you don't mind, I'm vegetarian, so I don't want to go to McDonald's or anything."

"I don't mind that you're vegetarian."

"Ha-ha. You know what I meant."

"Well, I'll miss out on my Happy Meal, but that's okay. Although I was really looking forward to that cheap plastic movie tie-in toy."

"If you want a toy, you can get one after we eat. But only if you're good."

Emma's joke helped me relax a bit as we turned toward Montague Street. It was such a nice day we decided to get sandwiches at the deli and take them to the Promenade. We sat on a bench and looked across the river at the Manhattan skyline straight ahead of us. It didn't look strange anymore without the Towers.

Emma took out the present right away and opened it. "It's beautiful!"

"Really?"

"Of course. It looks Chinese. Is it from China?"

"Yeah. I think. I mean, I bought it here. But from a Chinese woman my mom is friends with. My mom is even learning Chinese from her."

"That's so cool. I heard Chinese is the hardest language to learn. And French is bad enough, *n'est-ce pas?*"

"*Oui, mademoiselle.*"

And there we were talking to each other. Emma even told me she was kind of shy around boys, which was a huge relief to me.

"I don't have a lot of experience in that department," was how she put it.

"Me either. As you can probably tell," I admitted. "Unless I count all those stupid games of Spin the Bottle everybody played from sixth grade on."

"Then I get to count them too," she said with a shudder, "although I'd rather forget them."

I was even having fun, in between being stupidly nervous. I had so many questions about how to be with a girl. Correction—I have so many questions. And, of course, afterward, I had the thought that Isaac would never get to do that—sit on a bench with a maybe-girlfriend.

But at the time I was just glad I had ordered turkey, not something that would stick in my teeth and look disgusting, like egg salad.

———

I thought about Emma a lot after that. It really made me happier, gave me something else to focus on. I friended her on Facebook. No surprises there. Mostly just her faves, movies like *Easy A*, *Desperately Seeking Susan*—all respectable chick-flick choices. And photos of her, a lot with Olivia and Meredith, the three of them being a little goofy.

When she wasn't busy in the afternoons with some lesson, and I wasn't at Mom's school or at practice, we would get something to eat. Then we would talk on our cells later about our classes and our friends and bullshit about music, like why or why not the Beatles were geniuses. I wanted to get to know her. I was taking a course in Basic Emma.

"What's really important to you?" I asked her one night.

"Wow." She took a minute to think. "My friends?"

"They're something else, those two."

"We've been friends forever, since first grade. Actually, with Olivia, nursery school."

"Sort of like me and Sam."

"Funny how you just click with certain people, even if you're really different."

"I know."

"Let me ask *you* something," she said. "What about school? Like/dislike?"

"Overall, I put it in the plus column. I'm happy to be able just to concentrate on it again."

"You'll tell me if I'm asking something that's inappropriate or maybe painful?"

I couldn't help getting a little ticked off. "Look, please don't do that all the time."

"You mean be nice to you? I should stop being nice?" She was hurt. "I think it's really important to be nice to people. I can't stand it when someone is mean."

"I'm sorry. I'm just, well, tired of it."

"I understand. But I really can't take it when people get mad at me."

"I'm not mad, okay? Are we good?"

"We're good."

"So what were we talking about?"

"School. Is there any subject you actually like?"

"I actually like English."

"Like what? Reading novels?"

"Full disclosure? Even poetry."

"For real? Like who?"

"The usual suspects: e e. cummings, Dylan Thomas."

"Yeah?"

"Legit."

Emma laughed. "Well, I think you're very brave to admit it. And I feel honored that you trusted me with your darkest secret."

"Just don't let it get around." Then I asked her, "What happened, you know, with your birthday. The thing about the party?"

"It wasn't a thing. Like I said."

Now it was my turn to be hurt. "I just thought maybe something happened. You don't have to tell me if you don't want to."

I could hear her sigh over the phone. "You know how the girls were teasing me about my father?"

"Yeah."

"Well, sometimes he can be … difficult."

I had figured that from other stuff she'd said, but she had never come out and told me this directly before.

"How so?"

"It's like he needs everything to be perfect. If something isn't the way he thinks it should be, he blows up—at me, or my mom. And the 'shit happens' rule of life is that something always goes wrong."

"Like what?"

"Like one time I was eating pretzels in the car and got crumbs on the seat, and he was just furious, I mean bug-eyed furious at me. Or Mom says something he thinks is stupid when they're out with people. Once she mispronounced someone's name. Called her Mary instead of Maria or something earthshaking like that, and he yelled at her. It's always some little, meaningless thing."

"That's pretty harsh."

"Yeah. And you know? Sometimes, and I know this sounds bad, sometimes I even think he is a little crazy. Is that like a horrible thing to say about my own father?"

"No, no," I told her. "Not at all." I didn't think it was horrible to say. Only horrible that it might be true.

17

FIXER-UPPER

I had almost forgotten about Dad's scheme about moving to Lil's. He hadn't brought it up for weeks. But it turned out he hadn't dropped the idea. He started to mention it again at dinner. At some point that spring it seemed like every night when me, Mom, and Dad sat down to eat, all Dad wanted to talk about was fixing up Lil's house for us to live in. It got to where if I smelled something cooking, I began to think about the fight we were about to have. I was like one of Pavlov's dogs in that old experiment, drooling at the sound of a bell. Dad always started being all positive, saying how her house had an extra floor, or how much better the light was over there, or that the house was wider, or what a good "footprint" it had. And Mom's face would tighten up and she'd barely squeeze out a word in response. So Dad would just push harder.

"And the really great thing is that we can stay here in our house during the renovation so we don't have to live in the mess."

Mom answered by saying, kind of angrily, "You really seem to want this."

That really set Dad off. "It's not just for me! I think it'll be good for all of us. There's not that much to do. I already replaced the wiring and plumbing for Lil." Then one night he added, "So the worst part is over."

After he said those words we all just looked at each other.

"I didn't mean …," Dad said.

Me and Mom didn't say anything.

He went on. "Listen. I'm the one who knows about this stuff. And if I'm saying it's doable—"

"It's not just a case of that," Mom interrupted. "It's moving. It's leaving this house. It's a big life decision. All the experts say not to make big decisions after a … a tragedy."

Dad shook his head. "Please, spare me. I know what the 'experts' say. I believe we've both had our fill of that. And it's going on two years, Claire."

"Like that's a long time," I butted in.

Dad was gripping the end of the table. "Can you two just listen to me? Do you think I don't under-stand the emotional aspect of this? And maybe it will be easier to pack up Isaac's stuff if we're packing up everything else at the same time. Did you ever con-sider that?"

Mom put her head down and said very quietly that it seemed wrong, like we were giving ourselves a treat. "I feel like we'd be rewarding ourselves."

And Dad asked her if punishing ourselves instead was going to prove anything.

"I think we all deserve something good, positive in our lives," he said, and I could tell he was trying not to cry. He calmed himself down by talking details. "It needs some refinishing, painting. The floors should be scraped. And one of the bathrooms definitely has to be redone. We put a kitchen in the extension. Insulate it, of course. Then build a deck off it, so we can have access to the garden. Claire, we take the floor above, and Aaron, you could have a new room on the top floor."

And that made it real for me. He meant a room of my own, without Isaac. Up to then I hadn't even thought about taking down the wall Dad had built to separate our space. And suddenly I realized I'd have a whole new room to myself. A room Isaac never slept in, played in. A room that, supposedly, wouldn't remind me of him every minute.

I mean, when Isaac was around, there were a lot of times I wished he would go away so I'd have a place for myself, some privacy. But imagining my own room without him gave me such an empty feeling. I thought about stuff we'd done together. Like the time I got some Lego kit for my birthday, maybe I was nine, and he wanted to help me build it. Some fancy spaceship thing, I think, with tiny guys that have even tinier helmets you click onto their heads. And I told him he was too little and it was mine and to leave his grimy hands off it. But then I had some trouble putting it together—and he just figured it out. Didn't even have to look at the picture on the directions. He was amazing at that kind of thing. And he didn't say, "See? See? You couldn't do it and I could." Well, not much, anyway. Even as a little kid, he was a good person.

Dad was still talking. I started paying attention again when he was saying we could leave Lil's old kitchen downstairs for the rental.

Rental?

Mom said she wasn't thrilled by the idea of living with a stranger. But Dad said we could be picky and it might be nice to fill up the house.

I burst out, "You mean fill it with some kind of substitute Isaac?"

"Of course not!" Dad said.

But I couldn't stop myself. "That's just great. Let's just let anyone off the street live here, it doesn't matter who. Anybody'll do. We just need another warm body. You want something to fill up space? Let's get a dog—one of Crazy Harold's dogs, okay? He has a lot of them. We can take in some poor homeless doggy. We can name him Isaac."

I didn't bother to stick around to see how Mom and Dad took this. I got up from the table and ran down to my room. I remember them yelling something after me, but I wasn't listening to what it was. I just slammed my door and flopped down on my bed, stuck my earphones in, and tried to pretend I wasn't there.

18

BOY COLORS

Not only didn't I tell Emma, I didn't even let Sam know about what my Dad was thinking of doing. It seemed so wrong. I was afraid people would think he was bad or mean or something for wanting to get a new house after what happened. I talked with Orbach about it a little. But even in his office, I didn't want to have to go over and over it.

It was almost like right after Isaac died, when I couldn't talk to anybody. This time, I felt like, just when I was getting back to normal, just when I was getting my head above water, I was being pushed down under again.

Not telling became a bigger and bigger thing between me and my friends. It got to the point where when the group of us went out—me, Sam, Emma, Olivia,

101

and Meredith, because by then we were all friends—it was hard to be with them. We would go into the City together. I would stand outside on lower Broadway with Sam while the girls hit the stores. Sometimes we'd catch a movie at the Angelica or Sunshine. Or we'd just take over a couple of tables at a Starbucks and drink chai lattes. And I found myself, whenever we went downtown, thinking about Kim, the homeless girl I'd met. I felt kind of a connection to her. I would always sort of be looking for her. But I didn't think I could tell them about her, either. When there's something you're always trying not to say, it's like you choke on every word.

I see now how dumb that was—not talking to Sam and Emma, who actually gave a shit about me and maybe would have helped me through that time. But I had a way to help take my mind off Dad's plan: I started to stop by Mom's place even more after school to keep myself busy with the little kids.

I walked into the main classroom one day and saw Mom crouching down next to a boy. He was sitting in one of the small kid chairs, kicking his legs back and forth. I did a double take. It was Owen. It was wild seeing him there. Like I had the power to think something up and make it actually happen. Good old Orbach must have mentioned my idea to Owen's mom. She was there too, looking about as uncomfortable as I've ever seen anyone look, in her dress and heels, squished into the tiny chair next to his. Every time a new bunch of kids came in, she gave a nervous little shake, like just their being there got on her nerves. The kids didn't even notice her, just dropped their backpacks, crowded around the snack table, and grabbed some crackers and juice. Then they moved off into the back room. I went right over to Owen.

"Hey, Owen, my man."

"Aaron!" The goofy little kid started grinning and waving at me. He began to get up out of his chair, but his mother put her hand out to pull him back down. I thought: *what is this lady's problem?* I exchanged a look with Mom.

Owen started talking away a mile a minute.

"Aaron. Guess what? Dr. Orbach talked to my mom about coming here and she said *yes!*"

"Yes, well, I thought, if Dr. Orbach recommended it . . ." Owen's mother began to say.

"Rochelle, don't worry," Mom said softly. "Owen will be fine."

"Well, I had to take off from work to bring him. He wouldn't come with the babysitter."

Mom ignored this. She told Owen, "We have movement today with Lito. He's really nice. He's waiting to meet you."

"What's movement?" Owen asked.

"It's like dance. But, uh, freer."

Then he asked, "Who's Lito? What kind of name is that?"

The kid is HI-sterical.

Mom kept a straight face. "Good question," she said. "We'll have to ask." She stood up and held out her hand to Owen. "The other children are with him in the next room. Shall we go see what they're doing?"

Owen thought about it a second. His mother sat there like a statue. Then Owen got up and reached for my hand instead of Mom's. I felt all warm and fuzzy. He said he'd go. Old Rochelle, looking none too happy, got herself out of her chair. She was about to follow us, but Mom stopped her by saying very firmly something like, "Really, he'll be fine." That pretty much shocked her. I guessed people didn't usually dare to talk to her that way, but she obeyed Mom and froze in her tracks.

The tables had been pushed aside in the other room. The kids were grouped in a messy circle, their shoes in a pile in the corner. Lito, short and skinny, was standing in the middle of the circle, a drum under his arm. I brought Owen over to him. Lito gave him a big smile and a little bow. I tried to drop Owen's hand but he wouldn't let go of me. He'd probably been all excited about seeing me but hadn't thought about what it would be like to be in a strange place with a bunch of kids and grown-ups he didn't know. I kept trying to tell him it was okay, but the kid looked pretty terrified. So I led him to the edge of the room and sat down against a wall. Owen climbed into my lap to watch, but his little body was so stiff it was like holding a two-by-four.

The kids always seem to love their time with Lito. He usually has them act out some idea. He'll ask them to be different animals, like an elephant. Has them think about how an elephant would move and he beats the drum to help them get the feel. Then he switches the rhythm to something else, like a cat sneaking after a bird. They really get into it. I mean, you try to do that with older kids, they'll be too embarrassed or they'll laugh at you, give you attitude.

That day Lito asked them to make believe they were seeds. He took them through the whole nature thing—starting with the wind blowing, scattering those little seeds around. The kids floated around the room. Then they were supposed to be stuck in the dirt. They crouched down, trying to be still, but, of course, most of them couldn't stop wiggling. Next, Lito told them the rain was falling, and he beat his drum gently to imitate the sound. The kids started to stand up, like they were sprouting from the ground. And that was all leading up to the big moment when the sun came out and they became flowers, opening up, stretching out their arms, growing tall. I love a happy ending.

I reached around Owen and clapped like crazy. The kids looked so pleased with themselves. Owen had sat perfectly still through the whole thing. I wondered what he had thought of it.

"Wasn't that great, Owen?" I asked him.

"Sure," he said sarcastically. "Very special."

I didn't push it.

I walked him back into the main room for the next activity, another art project. It's amazing that everyone doesn't grow up to be artists, considering kids spend half their time coloring and pasting. Elspeth was handing out cardboard picture frames for the kids to decorate with feathers, sequins, markers, and glitter glue. During the year the teachers had taken photos of the kids, and each child could choose one to put in a frame. As soon as Owen realized what the deal was, he threw a fit. "There are no pictures of me!"

All the children turned to look at him. I was freaking out. It was my brilliant idea for Owen to come here, and it was becoming a disaster. But Mom wasn't worried. She came over and asked him if he knew what a Polaroid was.

He shook his head.

"I'll show you," she said, and went to one of the supply shelves and dug out her camera. I had to hand it to Mom. She came back over to Owen and didn't just take his picture, but asked Owen first if it was okay if she did. He nodded very seriously and looked up at her. Mom snapped away. All the kids were quiet as they watched the picture come out and the image appear. I mean, digital's great, but this was like a magic trick.

The photo was on the small side, but Owen was thrilled. He took a seat and began to pick things to put on his frame. I offered to help him, but he wanted to go solo. He knew just what to do. I saw Elspeth watching him, surprised and pleased. He reminded me a bit of Isaac the way he worked. He covered the frame in blue glitter, then stuck a red feather on the top and gold stars in the corners. I mean, it actually looked good— not like something a little boy would throw together. I remember exactly what it looked like because he gave it to me after it was finished.

But that day, before the paste holding the Polaroid inside had dried, Justin the Destroyer opened his mouth. "You put a red feather on yours. Red's a girl color!"

Elspeth had had enough. "There are no boy colors or girl colors, Justin. There are just colors."

It was a nice try. Owen ran out of the room into the hallway. I went after him. He scrunched himself down on the floor, his arms over his head. I tried to move his arms, but he pulled away from me. So I lowered myself down to sit next to him. Mom came out for a second and signaled to me that I should just stay there. I closed my eyes and tried to send positive energy over to Owen. But I felt totally useless.

It weighed me down how mixed up he was, how sad—and that there wasn't something I could do to fix it right then and there. I thought about when I'd feel bad after I had a fight with Isaac over something profoundly lame, like he'd touched one of my Power Rangers figures. Boy, brothers fight over dumb shit. I would say awful things to him. I mean, Isaac wasn't a strange kid like Owen, but he was sensitive. Always worried this friend or that one was mad at him. Got his feelings hurt really easily. I guess everyone does, but some people hide it better. Anyway, I would call him something really choice like a flaming asshole, and then he would just go silent and not say a word. That got to me. He knew it did. So I'd start saying funny, crazy things to make him laugh, and he would, and we'd both say we were sorry, and then it would be over.

I opened my eyes and looked up at the solar system Dad had painted on the ceiling, but for once it didn't give me any comfort. I sat there with Owen, praying for things to be okay again.

19

NO SHORTAGE OF ASSHOLES

I was beginning to think maybe I could talk to Emma about Dad and moving. I mean, she kept telling me about the messed up things *her* father did. But just when I decided to, Mom dropped her own—even bigger— bomb. Looking back, I guess I should have expected something like it.

It was a Saturday. Mom was making a humongous breakfast like she used to do on the weekend—eggs and pancakes. She had even gotten some bacon for me, a confirmed meat eater. And in the middle of cooking she burned herself because she grabbed for the pan without looking. And she hardly even got upset about it. She wasn't even bothered that Dad was across the street at Lil's, which should have given me a clue. She just told me to go get him.

Dad was crouched down outside inspecting the stoop. He was humming to himself, one of the old-ies he used to sing to me, the one about a guy being a great pretender, like he thinks he's fooling people he's not going crazy that his girlfriend or somebody isn't around anymore. Dad was so into what he was doing that I couldn't get his attention for a moment. When he finally looked up, he didn't even say, "Hi," just told me the steps needed to be redone. He sounded happy about it.

That made me suspicious. Suddenly Mom and Dad were both in a good mood. When I came back to the house, Mom was setting the plates out on the table. I asked her what was up.

She turned to me. "How do you mean?" she asked.

"Come on, Mom," I said angrily. "Is it the move? Did you guys not tell me you were going to go ahead with that?"

"I'm sorry," she said, reaching out to touch my arm. "I'm sorry I didn't say something sooner. But, yeah, probably, honey. I've been thinking it was a good thing to do."

"Good? You said it was wrong. You agreed with me. I thought you were on my side!"

"We're all on the same side."

"Bullshit."

"Aaron!"

"You said we shouldn't reward ourselves. Those were your words."

"It isn't a reward. It's a way to keep living."

I shook my head. "I can't believe you changed your mind just like that."

"You may change yours too when you know the reason," she said.

"What reason?" I shot back at her.

"I'll tell you when Dad's here."

I was going to say something more, but just then Dad walked in, washed up, and we all sat down to eat.

"Okay. So would someone please tell me what's going on?" I asked before I even took a bite.

Mom nodded and launched into a whole discussion—but not about moving. She started talking about China.

I couldn't figure out what in the world this had to do with the move or us or anything. "Uh, Mom. I thought you were going to explain about changing your mind."

"Just listen a minute. I'm getting to it," she said. "You know I'm friends with An Rui, right? Well, she was telling me about the government in China, how thirty years ago or so it instituted something called the one-child policy, dictating that people could have only one kid. Imagine. Recently things have gotten a little better. They've eased up on the rules a bit," she added, "but women are still sometimes actually forced to have abortions. Or, if they have another child, they're fined or punished—they might even have their houses burned down!"

I mean, that sounded harsh and all. But I didn't know what was going on. Why did she think I needed to know about this?

"Now, in China," she continued, "it's traditional to prefer sons. Well, the government didn't take that into account. So, what happened was, before most people had access to amnio or sonograms, if a couple's first child was a girl, they might try having a second, hoping it would be a boy and worth the risk. But if the second was a girl, they might not want to take a chance. So they wouldn't keep the baby. And they could try for a boy again. And, in other cases, if they had a baby born with a medical problem, something the family couldn't afford to take care of, they would also give up the baby."

"Not keep it? Give it up? What does that mean?" I asked.

"Well, that's a little hard for us to understand. There's no system in China for releasing a baby for adoption like there is here. So people would, uh, leave the babies some place."

"Excuse me?"

"Not in the middle of nowhere. In a place where they'd be found, where they knew a lot of people would pass by, like a market or train station or park. And then the babies would be brought to an orphanage."

"That seems really messed up," I said. Then a thought occurred to me. "Did An Rui leave a baby?" I asked. "Is that it? Did she, like, confess to you?"

"No, no. But she saw it—a baby found at a police station. She mentioned it because last week, at the flea market, a family came over to her table—a white mother and father with a little Chinese girl—and they asked if An Rui was from China and then which province. An Rui's from Hunan. They said the little girl was from another one. I can't remember the name."

I guess I'm pretty slow, but I couldn't begin to figure out what she was saying. "Mom, what are you talking about? What were they doing with this little Chinese girl?"

"She was their daughter, honey. They adopted her."

That's when the puzzle pieces came together. The *aha!* moment.

I sat there stunned. Dad started in explaining the situation more, but nothing was registering in my brain.

It wasn't until after that that I learned how many babies and families have been hurt by the law. Thousands—tens of thousands, maybe hundreds of thousands. And what is also so fucked up is not just the stupid policy. It's the whole way people still want boys more than girls—like there's a shortage of assholes. But the tradition in China was that when a girl married she went to live with her husband's family, so parents needed sons to help them when they got older. I guess it's hard to shake that kind of idea.

But that night, when Mom and Dad first brought it up, all I understood was that Dad was in on this little adoption scheme too. That the two of them had already worked everything out.

"Well, thanks a lot," I said sarcastically when they stopped talking. "I appreciate being kept up to speed on the conditions in China."

"Do you understand why we're telling you this?" Mom asked.

"Yeah, Mom. I'm not an idiot."

Mom sighed. "We thought you'd be happy about it."

"Are you kidding?"

"A-Team," Dad said, "would you just think about it?"

"Why should I?" I started ranting about how I thought what they were doing was wrong. I believe my phrase of choice was "un-fucking-believable."

"Calm down," Dad ordered.

I ignored him. "Moving wasn't enough for you? Now you're going to get another kid? Without talking to me? Without saying anything first? You don't give a shit about what I want!"

"Of course we do." Mom said. Then she repeated, sounding very sad, "We really thought you'd like the idea."

"No. You didn't think that. You couldn't believe that. All you really want is for me to say yes. I haven't even agreed to moving and this is way worse than that. Are you for real? It isn't even two years since Isaac died and already you're thinking of replacing him!"

"It's not like that," Dad said. "You know it's not like that!"

Mom was crying. "I need this or I don't know how I can stand it any longer."

Dad went over to Mom and put his arm around her.

I got up and left the room, shouting, "Go ahead and do whatever the hell you want!"

Without even thinking I ran downstairs and grabbed some money from the tin under my bed. Then I went out the gate. Dad was watching from the window and called after me, but I didn't stop. I felt like my whole life was being destroyed. That I didn't know who my parents were anymore. That I'd lost them as well as my brother.

20

THE "AI-AI-AI" BRAND

That was the day I saw Kim again. Even though I was always thinking, or hoping, I might run into her when I was in Manhattan with Sam or Emma, I had never actually done anything to make it happen. But after the scene at home, I got on the train with the idea of finding her. She had told me she didn't have anything to do with her family anymore. I was so confused, so angry, so fucked up, I thought maybe I had something to learn from her.

I felt better being out of my neighborhood. On the crowded sidewalks of the Lower East Side, everybody looked strange and had some story. Either they had pink hair, tattoos and piercings, or they were tourists in identical shirts with the name of their city and state written on them. I couldn't figure out if the matching clothes were so they could spot each other in case they got lost or some kind of hometown pride thing. *Iowa is in the house. Represent.* I remember having the idea—what if every family was required to have an official outfit? Ours would be something like Old Navy jeans and a "Develop Don't Destroy Brooklyn" T-shirt. Isaac would've found that HI-sterical.

I circled the blocks from Alphabet City—Avenues A, B, C, D—to Broadway to Houston to St. Mark's. I described Kim to a few of the people selling stuff on the street, asked if they'd seen her, like I was searching for a long-lost relative. I went into Cheap Jack's and Screaming Mimi's and a couple of the bodegas to look for her in there. I was really self-conscious, felt like everyone was staring at me, and I sometimes wound up running out of the stores like I had stolen something. I was kicking myself for not having gotten Kim's phone number or e-mail or address, some way of getting in touch with her. Although chances were good she didn't have any of those. And, of course, I didn't even know her real name.

I was starting to feel pretty crazy, going around and around the same streets. I stopped at a luncheonette to get a cup of coffee, hoping having something to hold on to would calm me down. My cell rang, and I turned it off without even checking who it was. I figured it was Mom or Dad or maybe Orbach calling to find out why I'd missed our appointment.

Near Cooper Square I saw a guy selling some cheesy paintings of famous places in New York—the Empire State Building, the Twin Towers—laid out on a blanket. I asked him if he'd seen a really skinny girl, around my age, with blond hair and bad teeth.

He shook his head but kept his eyes on me. Then he asked, "You looking for someone to hook you up?"

I realized that he thought I wanted to buy drugs. My first reaction was—not me. But it took maybe a second to ask myself why not.

Glancing around to make sure no one else was near us, he gave me the number of a house on St. Mark's. "Tell them Rick said it was cool."

I crossed Second Avenue and started studying every building. Most of them had stores on the bottom floor, and some had tiny restaurants. In front of the address Rick had given me, these three macho types were sitting on the stoop. I was scared shitless to go over to them. I didn't know what I should say, how you're supposed to do that—score drugs. I decided not to mention anything about drugs, just ask about Kim.

When I did, one of the guys, whose biceps were so huge the sleeves of his T-shirt stretched tight around them, squinted up at me. "Friend of yours?"

"Kind of. You know her?"

"I think I seen her around."

"Yeah? You wouldn't—I mean—would you know, like, where she is?"

"That one? Gotta be somewheres."

There was something really nasty in the way he said it, so I told him thanks anyway.

"Hey, you was the one asking." He stared at me. "You don't look like her usual type a friend."

"No? How's that?"

"Her usual kind is fucked up." He laughed like that was really funny and repeated it. "Totally fucked up!"

The two other guys nodded and smiled and bumped their knuckles against his.

Then he stopped laughing and said, "How come you asking us, anyways?"

"Rick sent me." It sounded like a line from a bad movie. The man stood up and motioned for me to follow him up the steps. "Wait by the door." He pointed to the two other guys. "Lee and Marco'll keep you company. Hawk's gonna help you out."

Hawk? I thought. *Really?* Of course he'd have a name like that. I climbed up the stairs as he went into the building, then leaned against the iron handrail and tried to look casual, like buying drugs was nothing epic, something I did all the time, but my heart was pounding so loud I couldn't hear the traffic. The other two guys were scanning the block, watching for cops. I thought briefly about what would happen if I got arrested—what it would do to Mom and Dad—and that maybe I should just run like hell, but it was like I was paralyzed.

As I stood there I even told myself that this is what I wanted—to do something that cut me off from Mom and Dad. I concentrated on looking at the stores and people across the street. There was a Japanese restaurant and a stand selling bags and sunglasses and a frozen yogurt place and a palm reader and a shoe store. A girl walked by and stopped to look at the shoes in the window. She was really thin and nodding her head to the music on her iPod. And I recognized her. It was Kim.

That got me moving. I ran down the stoop, pushed past the two lookouts, and crossed St. Mark's Place, calling her name. I was a little afraid the guys were going to follow me, but there were too many people, and I was making too much noise.

Kim didn't react. Of course, she couldn't hear me because of the headphones. I went up right next to her and waved my hand next to her face. She turned away from the window and looked at me blankly, slowly removing an earpiece.

"Kim. It's me. Aaron. We met a few weeks ago?" I was grinning like a crazy man. I think I must have looked like the friggin' Cheshire Cat.

I wasn't sure she remembered me, but she said, "Oh, yeah. Hey, dude. Wanna chill?" Just like she had the last time. But this time I said, "Definitely."

"You got any money, man?"

"About twenty bucks."

Without another word, she reached out to grab my hand. I noticed a tattoo of a woman on the inside of her arm. She told me it was the Virgin of Guadalupe. "She protects me."

"Like your saints?"

"Better. She's number one."

We started walking toward Tompkins Square Park. So I had done it. Found her. And now that I had, I hadn't a clue what to say to her. Finally I asked, "How's Rosa?"

"Who?"

Clearly it didn't ring any bells. I repeated her story about the movie theater and the brother and the coat she gave away. She shrugged. "Whatever, man."

We were walking along Avenue A when out of nowhere I felt a tap on my shoulder. I practically jumped a couple of feet. I turned to see one of the lookout guys.

At least six-two, with straight black hair tied back in a ponytail.

"Hey, dawg. You forget something?"

I was too scared to speak.

Kim answered him. "It's okay, Lee. He's with me."

Lee gave me a dirty look but let us keep going. I started breathing again. We reached the park, which is always a little scuzzy looking. I didn't know what to say, so I made some stupid joke about were we going to the park to play baseball?

Kim stopped and stared at me, narrowing her eyes. Then she said, "I remember you. You're the funny dude."

"Not me. Wrong guy. A case of mistaken identity."

"No. It's you. Sometimes I don't remember stuff. But I know you." And then she put her face up to mine like she was going to kiss me. I pulled away, but she asked me, "So you wanna do anything? We could go over to those trees over there." She was so casual about it—like she was asking if I wanted to watch TV—that I didn't understand right away she meant sex. I mean, it's not like I didn't, or don't, think about sex. But the idea of doing it in a public place with Kim was not exactly a turn-on.

She didn't seem to care that I said no. Instead, she led me to a small red-brick building that stank of piss even though the bathrooms inside were boarded up. We stood there for a minute, and then who should walk up but Hawk.

"Hey," he said to me. "If it isn't the invisible man. One minute you see him, then—*poof*—you don't."

I started to explain, but Kim cut me off. "Just give me the twenty." Which I did. In a second, she had turned to

Hawk, made an exchange, and Hawk headed off. Kim started walking in the opposite direction and said to follow her, and I did that too, like I was on automatic pilot.

We walked away from the park, past vacant stores, apartment houses with graffiti on the brick and doors, and seedy-looking bars. Kim knew where to go. We wound up in a small garden on Avenue D, a place that just didn't seem to belong in the middle of all that ugly. Somebody was really taking care of it—there were all kinds of trees and bushes and clean paths made up of little pebbles. But no one else was there then, and the trees hid us from people walking by on the sidewalk. Kim sat on a bench. She opened her hand to show me two small green pills. She held one out to me.

"You'll like this," she said. "It's a good high."

I guess I didn't care what happened. I wasn't thinking about anything. I didn't want to think about anything. So I sat down next to her and reached for the pill. It looked like regular medicine, like something I'd take for a headache, except it had some strange design etched on it. I asked her what it was.

She looked at it more closely. "That's the 'Ai-Ai-Ai' brand, brother," she told me with a laugh. "It sounds like Spanish, but Lee told me it's the Chinese word for love." She pointed to the pattern. "See that? Those four marks on the bottom? That's supposed to be the heart. Maybe because … this stuff? You have to have a strong heart to take it. You don't have a bad heart or nothing? Not that a kid would, right?"

It was so weird her asking me that. I sometimes wondered if all those medical tests Mom and Dad made me get after Isaac died—to see if I had the same problem he had—had missed something. Maybe my heart did have something wrong with it like Isaac's and the doctors hadn't found it. No one had ever found it in Isaac's.

Kim popped the pill in her mouth and reached for my coffee to swallow it down. And so I put mine on my tongue, not even realizing she had never told me what it was I was taking. Kim handed my cup back and I took a sip. We just sat there for a while, and I was beginning to think the whole thing was a scam when I began to feel really excited, crazy, like fireworks were going off inside me. I jumped up and told Kim I wanted to run.

It gets a little hazy from there. I do remember being on a swing and then falling off and some people yelling at me, so I guess we were back in the park. And then being surrounded by a lot of lights and crystals. The sound of car horns. And then seeing a gold statue of some kind of god with a million arms that seemed to be reaching out to me. Unless I mixed that up with Kim's Virgin.

We must have been heading downtown because the next thing I remember is a church and behind it crooked old tombstones that seemed to be pointing straight toward Ground Zero, which was pretty spooky. And then we were right by the Brooklyn Bridge. I wanted to go over it, but Kim said it was too big, too high. It freaked her out.

I kept trying to get her to go with me, but she was almost crying, so I quit doing that. But for some reason it seemed so important to get onto the bridge, to see the city from up there, that I walked away from her. I felt really sad looking back at her, though. Strange, because I hardly knew her. I told her I'd come back to see her.

She turned to leave but then stopped and gave me a blessing: "May Our Lady protect you."

I watched her move slowly uptown until she blended into the crowd, and I couldn't tell which one she was. I stood there for a while, people bumping into me. Then I managed to find the wooden walkway and started to cross the bridge.

I hadn't walked over it for years—maybe as far back as elementary school when our class went there for a trip. I guess we were studying New York City. Second grade. We each had to make a building out of cardboard boxes. I was assigned to do a library. When Dad heard that, he got kind of nutso and decided I should make something special, not some crummy branch library, but the main one on Forty-Second Street, the one with the huge staircase and the lions out front. I remember we even bought little plastic lions to glue on. Dad helped a lot, which is to say, Dad made it.

I climbed up until I got to the midway point between Manhattan and Brooklyn. A tugboat pushing a barge was passing on the river below me. It was pretty amazing being there between the water and sky, with the sun shining through the crisscrossed cables and the flag on top waving in the wind. I faced south toward the Statue of Liberty and stretched out my arms. It was like I was holding on to Manhattan with my right hand, Brooklyn with my left. Like I *was* the Bridge.

I felt great for about a couple of minutes. Then I started to feel like shit. My jaw hurt, I had never been so thirsty in my life, and my clothes were sticking to me I was sweating so much. I didn't want to go home, but I didn't know what else to do. I checked my pockets. I had no money and I must have lost my MetroCard. So I kept walking—through Brooklyn Heights to the Middle Eastern and antiques and clothes stores on Atlantic, and then past the old housing projects, over the canal and around the warehouses to Fourth Avenue with its gas stations and flat-fix places and new glass-box condos, and finally up the hill to the Slope. It seemed like I was walking forever, like I was never going to get back.

21

RISK, SORRY, TROUBLE, LIFE

I let myself in downstairs, stripped off my clothes, took a quick shower, and locked my door before crawling into bed. I felt like the living dead. I was half aware of Mom and Dad tapping on my door and calling my name. I grunted in response, but couldn't speak if I'd wanted to. I fell asleep listening to their voices. When I woke up, it was about 9:30. For a minute I was confused whether it was 9:30 in the morning or at night. But then I realized it was light out. It was the next day. Sunday.

I lay there awhile, kind of a blank. Mom was outside my door, asking if I was okay. I finally gave her an angry yes, and soon after I heard her and Dad go out.

Suddenly I felt like I had all this extra energy and would explode if I didn't do something. I jumped out of bed and started pacing around. I went into Isaac's half of the room. I was crying. I didn't even realize it at first. Like water was dripping on my hands and I couldn't figure out where it was coming from. I mean, really crying—like I hadn't done since I was maybe six years old—and couldn't stop. And before I even knew what I was doing, I started to gather up Isaac's things: board games, clothes, comics, books, figures, *Magic* cards, a huge container of Lego pieces. It was like I had this mission—get rid of it all. I was talking to myself like a street crazy. Saying things like, "He's dead. You sell dead people's stuff. Mom taught me that. We're moving? Right? Then why the hell should we bother lugging this shit across the street? They want to get a new kid? Better make room for her. Don't want any of Isaac's crap in the way."

I began to have a clear idea in my head of how to organize everything. I placed the comics in neat piles: *Animal Man, X-Men, Punisher.* I put the *Lord of the Rings* stuff together. The toys and puzzles. Then the clothes. He had all these promotional T-shirts he had taken from Dad: Altabef Realty, Fine Floors by Freedberg, Tartack Heating and Cooling.

I unlocked the gate and started hanging the shirts outside on the railing in front of the house. I ran down to the basement and carried up a folding table and arranged things on it, just like at the flea market. I made a stack of the games: *Risk, Sorry, Trouble, Life.* What a list, right? Me and Isaac used to fight sometimes playing them. Little kids hate to lose. I guess no one likes it much.

There was a ton of books crammed in his bookshelf. Some of them had been mine. I found most of the ones in that series where you read about adventures and can choose the ending. What a joke. Like any of us gets to choose.

I worked up a sweat setting everything up, going back and forth from the house. Those books were heavy! When I finished, I was really pleased with the job I'd done. It looked pretty good. Neater than stuff I did usually was. I stood looking it over for a while. I felt calmer. A man with a baby hanging from him in one of those cloth papoose things stopped by and asked if I had any little kid books, but I told him I wasn't open yet.

I went back inside and found some poster board left over from a science fair project or something and a roll of string. I sat on the stoop and made up a list of prices using a Sharpie, then tied it to the railing. A lady and her little boy, around seven or eight, came over. The kid started to lift up the box of Lego blocks and it got me nervous.

"Hey, be careful with that!" I guess I kind of yelled at him. The lady gave me a dirty look, and the two of them walked away. After a little while some nerdy-looking guy started picking through the Tolkien posters.

"How much?" he asked me.

I pointed to my sign. "Ten bucks. Each."

He gave me a look. "That's way too much."

That really bothered me. "You think because I'm a kid you can cheat me?"

"Hey, take it easy, guy." He shook his head and left.

No one else came for a long time. I was straightening things out some more when Mom and Dad started walking up the block, carrying bags from the bookstore. They stopped when they saw what I'd done. They didn't say anything right away. Mom came over and stared at the stuff for a while. Finally she looked at me and asked, "Isn't this Isaac's?"

"Yeah."

Then Dad said. "All of it? You're selling all his things?"

"So?" I practically screamed at him. "Why not? Who needs them anymore? There won't be room for them, anyway, in the new place. With the new kid."

"Aaron, quiet down," Dad said. "We could store everything in Lil's basement. There's plenty of room."

"What's the sense in that?"

Mom said that maybe I should just wait a little.

"How long did you wait after Lil died?"

Mom looked really hurt. She started to say how that was different, but I didn't want to hear it.

"Think about this," she said to me. "Are you really sure you don't want to keep at least some of it? Something maybe even to show your own children?"

I grabbed an *Annihilation* comic and held it up. "This, maybe? You think *this* is going to help me remember my brother? You think if I ever have children they'd want old shit from someone they never knew? Because, let's face it, they're never going to know him."

Mom was finding it hard to talk, but she gave it another shot. "Have you thought this through?"

I went berserk. "I can't believe you can ask me that. You're asking *me* if *I've* thought it through?"

We all became aware that people were staring at us. Dad told me again to cut it out. "We're just trying to stop you from doing something you might regret later."

"Maybe you should take your own advice."

He was trying to keep his voice steady. "Let's just pack this up and go inside. We need to talk to you about what happened yesterday. Your disappearing like that. Quite a stunt."

I gave him some kind of nasty answer. Dad ignored it and bent down to pick up a carton of books.

"Put it down," I told him.

"I don't like your tone, Aaron," he said, but he replaced the books on the ground. When he stood back up I could see he was crying. Mom asked if I had sold anything yet. She seemed relieved when I said no.

Mom took a last look. "It actually looks nice the way you arranged all this," she said, really softly. Then she and Dad went into the house.

I sat on one of the steps, convincing myself that I was doing the right thing. A car pulled up, double-parked, and an older woman and man got out. They creeped me out, the way they were touching everything. The woman went over to the pile of games.

"I'll take these, but only if they have all the pieces. If I buy them all, how about ten dollars for the lot?"

She started to lift the cover off the *Monopoly* box when I stood up and shouted at her to stop. "It's a mistake. I can't sell those. My brother changed his mind. It's his stuff and he changed his mind."

The two of them stared at me like I'd gone totally insane, which I guess I had. "Dearie," the woman said, "you're not going to get very far with that attitude." They shook their heads and got back in their car. I watched them drive away and then turned back to look at what I'd laid out. Pieces of Isaac. And then I tore the price list off the railing. I grabbed a handful of the shirts and carried them back into my room and went outside again. I hauled the carton of books that Dad had started to move back inside. Dad must have been watching me because when I got back out he was there, gathering up the Hobbits and other action figures. We worked together, not talking, until everything was put away.

22

A MINOR CORRECTABLE CONDITION

After we were done, I was totally exhausted. I slowly climbed up the stairs after Dad. Mom was lying on the living room couch, reading one of the books from the pile she and Dad had just brought home. I looked at the covers. The word "adoption" was in all of the titles.

I meant to apologize, but instead said something like, "So you're going ahead with this."

Mom put her book down. "Let's talk about that later, Aaron. What we need to discuss now is yesterday. Where in hell did you go? What did you do?"

For a second I thought about telling them what I actually did, but figured it would just cause more problems. So I lied and said, "Nowhere in particular. I just walked around and stuff."

Dad started to speak but I cut him off.

"What does it matter? I went into Manhattan, okay? It's like I go crazy or something and just have to get away!"

"I'm sorry everything's so hard on you, but that's no excuse," Mom said. "When that happens, talk to someone. If you don't want to come to us, you have your friends or Dr. Orbach."

I shook my head. "When I feel like that, talking doesn't seem like it's going to work."

"But it could be dangerous, wandering around the streets all alone."

"Mom, I'm not a child," I answered. But I was thinking about Kim and how she was about as old as I was and living out on the street, and how maybe fourteen or fifteen wasn't exactly the time to go solo. I remembered when me and Sam and the girls had talked about special ages, what they meant. Whatever fourteen was, it wasn't the age of independence.

We went on talking in circles for a while. They kept asking questions and I kept not telling them anything.

"Look," Dad finally said. "This is getting nowhere. I just want you to promise that next time you feel like you need to go somewhere, I don't care if you're angry at us or upset with us or whatever it is, you let us know. And you keep your phone on. So we can get in touch with you."

I think we all knew that wasn't much of a solution, but none of us had any energy left to fight it out. Maybe, before Isaac died, if I'd done something like that, they would have grounded me. But after, they couldn't bring themselves to punish me.

Mom said we still needed to talk about the baby. "I know it seems we sprang it on you, but this might be the best thing for all of us. It can help us. It makes me feel a little hopeful. It just raises me out of myself, thinking about having another child in my life."

It was the first time since Isaac died that I'd heard Mom sound like that.

"It's not that I don't want that for you," I told her, "but I can't keep up with everything that's going on. I feel like I'm on a moving sidewalk, like at the airport, and I can't get off. There's too many things happening too quickly. Too many things changing."

Dad said, "Maybe things need to change."

"But why take in someone else's kid?" I asked.

"Someone else would give birth to her," Mom said. "We would be her family."

"But why China? Why not get a local kid who at least looks like us?" I guess I was thinking of someone like Kim—younger, before things got really bad for her.

"But that's not important," Dad explained. "That's not the issue. We want a child. We want a girl, because a girl will not be Isaac. And China's almost a sure bet for a girl. And your mom has a feeling about it, like this is what's right for us."

Then Mom added, "We need to let you know that we're asking for a child with a minor medical condition."

"What!" Were they crazy? "What does that mean?"

"Please, Aaron," she said. "Don't worry. Nothing serious. It could be just a birthmark or something correctable that just needs some physical therapy."

"But what if there's something else wrong?"

"You mean with her heart." She looked straight into my eyes. "We won't take a child with a heart condition. Or anything else like that. We couldn't."

Dad started to explain that this way we'd get a child sooner. "The process for special needs kids is expedited. We're not getting any younger. It will take time anyway, but we don't want to wait years."

I wasn't convinced. "But what if they're lying to you? What if—"

Mom reached for my arm and squeezed it. "We have to trust the adoption agency. And the Chinese."

They had thought it through without me. It was like we were in separate worlds. I didn't say anything more, just pulled away from Mom, grabbed one of the books and took it downstairs with me. It was called something like *Are Those Kids Yours?* I started to go through it. It had all these ways of how you could deal with stupid things people said to you because maybe you and your kids were different races and people didn't think you were a "real" family, and how you went about adoption in the first place and all the hoops you had to jump through before it could happen. All sorts of papers and tests you needed to get. A million nosy questions that needed to be answered. I realized that this whole adoption thing wasn't going to be too easy if you needed a bunch of books to tell you how to handle it. I saw what Dad meant about it taking time.

At least I had some breathing room.

23

THE PEOPLE IN YOUR NEIGHBORHOOD

I checked my phone and saw Sam had left like a million messages. When I got back to him, he told me Mom and Dad had called him on the day they couldn't find me. I think the way he described it was that they were scared out of their friggin' minds. He wanted to come over and talk about it and I said okay, even though I didn't really feel like seeing anyone.

We sat in my kitchen eating microwave popcorn. Extra butter. Between mouthfuls, Sam kept asking me to tell him what happened, where I'd gone. I didn't want to tell him about Kim. I don't know why exactly. I think I wanted—needed—to hold on to my secrets. Something that was only mine. And maybe the tiny part of my lizard brain that was actually thinking about escaping for real didn't want to let anyone in on that.

I know I didn't want to tell him about trying what, I had figured out, must have been Ecstasy. I knew it was beyond stupid. I suppose I was kind of embarrassed for Sam to know that about me.

So I just gave him the same story I'd given Mom and Dad about going into Manhattan and not doing much of anything.

"And quit worrying about it," I told him with as much conviction as I could manage. "Nothing's the matter."

Sam gave me one of his slow nods and said something sarcastic like, "Clearly."

That pissed me off. "Why do you always think you know better? You can be wrong sometimes. Maybe you don't know me like you think you do."

"Okay," he said, starting to get angry right back at me. "So I don't know everything. But I've been your best friend since kindergarten and I *do too* know you. I know we used to tell each other shit."

"Yeah. We did. But you didn't lose a brother."

"No. No, I didn't. You're right about that. That's historically accurate."

I ignored his tone. "I've changed. Maybe you don't know what I'm feeling. Maybe I see things differently now. See the world differently. That there's more out there than maybe we've ever thought about."

Sam let out a little laugh. "More? Of course there's more. There better be more or someone's been lying to us our whole lives. But what more do you mean?"

"I don't know. Maybe I just mean not the same. What does it matter? Why do I have to answer your questions?"

"You don't. You don't have to do anything. You can do what you want. Hang out in Manhattan. Run off with the Big Apple Circus. Become a roadie for the Foo Fighters."

I couldn't help cracking a smile. "Look, it's just hard for me to talk about this. Because … I was such an idiot."

"Hey, we've done all sorts of stupid shit together," he said, seeming less mad. "Remember back in fifth grade? When we had the whole class yell 'Superbad!' on cue and the principal happened to be passing by?"

"Oh, yeah," I groaned. "I think our parents were glad we went to different schools after that."

"Yet here we still are."

I nodded. "Here we are."

"So who can you tell if you can't tell me?"

He was right, of course. And so I told him about the day with Kim.

Sam was a bit shocked. "That's heavy-duty, man."

"I know. I said."

"Still, Aaron, be real here. Do you think you're the only teenager in New York City, in this God-blessed America, who has tried drugs?"

"Of course not. I mean, have you?"

"Ye-ah. What do you think? There were oh-so-many lonely nights when you weren't around. And some other people were. Who were generous enough to introduce me to the friendly neighborhood pusher, the nice man who hangs out in the schoolyard at night because he knows that's where a lot of kids go."

"It makes me think of that song from *Sesame Street*. The one about the people who live in the neighborhood."

Sam laughed. "Right. The mail carrier, the police officer, the firefighter, the drug pusher."

"So what did you use?"

"Mostly pot. Went to a party in some kid's parents' loft once where they had shrooms."

"So who's not being upfront? You've been keeping stuff from me."

"I don't do it much. But, yeah, I guess I have. Touché." He grabbed another handful of popcorn. We sat for a while not talking. Then Sam asked, "So you think you'll be seeing that Kim girl again?"

"I don't know. I haven't thought that far."

"Maybe it's not the best idea."

"Probably not."

"You still want to?"

I shrugged. "She was just there that first time, you know? When I needed to get away. Now she's part of it. The wanting to do something different."

"Something dangerous?"

"Maybe." I shook my head. "It sounds so dumb. Like 'Danger is my middle name.'"

"Yeah, well, you lived up to it. What you did was pretty out there. Hanging with that girl—"

"It's not her, it's the creeps she's with."

"It's her too."

"But I feel really bad about her."

Sam nodded. "It sucks."

"That it does."

"Why do you think you went back looking for her? What set you off? I mean, why do that instead of seeking the wisdom of yours truly? Or solace in the arms of the lovely Emma? Or the paid services of your shrink?"

And then—it was such a relief I couldn't believe I hadn't done it earlier—I told him what was going on at home; that, on top of moving, Mom and Dad were planning to adopt a baby. I put in all the negatives I could think of about the adoption. How they were replacing Isaac, getting some strange kid who didn't look like us, that my parents were completely and totally messed up, that the kid was going to have something wrong with her, how the whole thing would be a disaster. When I finished, I waited for Sam to say something to back me up. But he didn't. What he said was that he liked the idea. He thought it was cool.

"You know, I could really get behind this whole Chinese sister thing."

That got me pissed again. I had just wanted Sam to say, *Yeah. Be angry. Be mad at the world. You know the truth. Your parents are wrong.* But he didn't.

"See—I told you you wouldn't get what I was feeling," I was practically screaming at him. "It's so wrong— to move on, to change. It's like disrespecting Isaac. Going on with our lives, bringing another kid into them. Forgetting about Isaac."

Sam tried to interrupt, but I kept right on going. "If I died, how long would it be before they forgot about me, old what's-his-name?"

Sam yelled back, "Oh please! You think your parents have forgotten Isaac? You think if something happened to you that they'd just merrily go on their way? Boy, you are making no sense!"

"Okay, so maybe that's over the top. But can't you hear what I'm saying? Why do they need to try to fill the hole? It's like saying it *can* be filled. That's not right."

Sam shook his head. "Your parents are really hurting. Maybe this will help them. Help you, even."

"Why should we be helped? Isaac died! We *should* be unhappy!"

"For how much longer?"

"Dead is forever."

Sam stood up and got himself a drink of water from the kitchen sink to calm down. I'm lucky he didn't give up on me.

"I'm sorry, man," I said.

And Sam, being Sam, said it was NBD. Then he even joked, "Your sister is sure to be a vast improvement over my own biological sibling. The one I affectionately call Pain in the Ass."

It's true. Sam's little sister is obnoxious, just like that D.W. character on *Arthur*.

But that got me wondering about what my sister would be like. Worrying that maybe she'd be a loser—stupid or ugly or that there'd be something really wrong with her, something they wouldn't tell us about before it was too late. That she'd be sick. Or get sick.

"What if she's in worse shape than they say? And then something happens?" I asked Sam. "How would we deal with another dead kid?"

"Dude. There are no guarantees. Last time I checked, nothing in life comes with a Get Out of Jail Free card. But why not take the chance? Look at it this way—you get to be a big brother again. You really rock at that."

"Yeah. I was so good at it I let Isaac die."

"You know you didn't. You know you loved him."

Happy memories of Isaac were still painful then. Lately it's gotten a little easier. But that day, when

Sam said that, one thing did pop into my head. It was the first time I went with Mom and Dad and Isaac to Six Flags. Maybe I was nine or ten and Isaac seven or eight. I had been hounding Mom and Dad for weeks to go. And I'd recruited Isaac to nag them too, even though I don't think he really understood what the big deal was. So we drove out to New Jersey, and when we got there Isaac couldn't believe how great it was. But most of the rides he was too short for, or Mom and Dad were afraid to let him go on, and he was crying, looking up and seeing me on them. So I went on some of the baby rides with him and told him that they were really the best ones, anyway. I don't know if he totally believed me, but we had fun. And then at the end of the day we went on Congo Rapids. The two of us screaming and getting totally soaked. He was so happy. When we got back in the car to go home we were still wet. Isaac was completely wasted, and he fell asleep against me in the back seat of the car. I remembered how cold it felt with his wet clothes on me, but I didn't push him off. And then it felt warm and peaceful, and I fell asleep too. That was such an amazing day.

But what also came to mind were all the times I'd been a dick. I told Sam that the very day Isaac died I'd gotten mad at him for forgetting his MetroCard.

"Come on. You can't beat on yourself for not being perfect. Or, actually, you can, but, man, you'd be at it nonstop. I mean the clothes, the hair, the subpar video game skills … I could go on."

"Don't try to make me laugh."

"You thought I was kidding?"

I did laugh, but what Sam said really got to me. He had been fooling around, but the truth was I *had* been beating on myself for a long time. And I hadn't exactly been going easy on other people, either.

We made more popcorn and started to talk about other things, like what we were going to do for the summer. Sam's parents could be pretty hardass. They'd sent him away to camp every summer since he was nine years old. But this year he wasn't going to Camp Wigwam. I always thought it was so cute, really, his going to camp. I imagined him in the middle of the Adirondacks. The mountains—a lake—insects. The complete nature package. And where is Sam in all this? Sam is lying down on a bunk in a cabin reading some three-volume biography of Franklin Delano Roosevelt, ignoring the counselor who is trying to get him to go canoeing or hiking or some other totally un-Sam-like activity. It was always hard for me to picture Sam sitting around a campfire—almost as hard as it was for me to imagine Sam passing around a joint.

Sam had finally told his parents he was never, under any circumstances, spending that much time outdoors ever again. Especially not at a place that put a Kraft slice and ketchup on an English muffin and called it pizza.

That summer he wanted to go to a filmmaking program in Manhattan, but it cost too much. His parents said they'd give him half the money if he came up with the rest.

"They're not thinking long term," he said half seriously. "I'll pay them back ten times over when I become famous. The next Alfred Hitchcock. The next Ingmar Bergman. Or at least the next Judd Apatow."

"And I can say I ate popcorn with you when you were just Sammy from the block."

"And I'll always remember the little people. All those ordinary, untalented people I rose above," Sam said in his false sincere voice.

"So, Great One, what are you going to do for money?"

Sam made a pained face. "Get a job?"

"I know it's quite a comedown for you, but that's what I'm doing."

I had already told Mom I would work at the school. I was beginning to worry that wasn't such a good idea because I was still so angry at her and Dad, but I didn't have any other options and couldn't imagine just chilling all summer. Of course, we wouldn't be taking any kind of vacation the way we used to. We hadn't even been able to think about it for two years. And now we had to save up for the move. And maybe a trip to China.

Sam and I talked about possible things he might do. The list was limited, and there was nothing that paid very well or that he didn't have a sarcastic comment about. I said maybe he could be an assistant at a day camp.

"You mean like what you do? Working with, you know, those things that cry and whine and need their asses wiped? What do you call them—*children?*"

"I thought you were the one who just said it's a good idea for me to get a little sister?"

"The operative word here is 'you'—*you're* getting the little sister."

"You don't like kids?"

"I like the concept. The whole childhood thing—crayons, macaroni and cheese, Batman backpacks—that's all good. But the individual child units I have a problem with."

"It's weird. I don't want some strange kid in my family, but I really do like kids. They're so, well, sincere. And they'd *love* you."

Sam seemed horrified. "Let's move on, shall we?"

At some point Dad came home whistling another way-way oldie like *I'll Get By* and went into the kitchen. He looked pretty grungy after working over at Lil's, but he was really upbeat. He started to tell us about all he needed to do over there, and, almost without thinking, Sam asked if he needed help.

Dad was stunned for a second there. "Are you serious, Sam?"

"Yeah. I think I am."

"Well, all right then. I can always use a good man."

I mouthed the word "money" to Dad, hoping Sam didn't see. Dad took the hint.

"Of course I'll pay you something. A little something."

Sam smiled. "Done deal."

And it seemed like a good deal, too, until I remembered how, if the worst hadn't happened, it would have been Isaac helping out Dad. And I'd feel a whole lot different about moving to Lil's.

24

STUFF THAT MIGHT COME IN HANDY

After that talk with Sam I started to remember more about Isaac, things I hadn't let myself think about before. It still was hard, but it was like I was trying to hold onto him: how he talked, stuff we'd done together. And then, on one of those weekends when I didn't know what to do with myself, I decided to go to a place he had really liked. The museum that was probably his favorite place in the whole city. The big one—the Metropolitan. Like I'd feel closer to him there. Lil and Mom and Dad had dragged me to it a few times. And in third grade my teacher made us go on this field trip to look at the medieval stuff. Knights and armor and like that, which I guess was pretty cool. But Isaac really loved everything about the Met.

I took the 4 train to Eighty-Sixth Street and then realized I had no idea which way to walk. I asked directions from some lady who had on these huge sunglasses and whose hair was so blond it was almost white. Bad choice. She gave me attitude because I didn't know exactly where the Met was. I mean, please. I'm a kid, or sort of a kid. I don't understand why some people have to go out of their way to give other people a hard time.

Turned out the museum wasn't far, just a few long blocks away on Fifth Avenue, blocks filled with old apartment buildings and fancy stores. When I got to Fifth, I was right by Central Park. There was a low stone wall along it and beyond that the trees. It was really beautiful, all that green. Up ahead I could see the museum, looking like a big, white palace, with fountains on either side of it. A huge stone staircase led up to the entrance, and hanging over it were these giant banners advertising the exhibits. The steps were jammed with people sitting, standing, going up and down, eating, taking pictures. Some kids a few years older than me were huddled in a small group. They were wearing matching T-shirts. This time it was a religious thing: The shirts all said *Bible Crusade.*

I couldn't afford the "suggested" entrance price, but the guy at the desk said that was okay when I showed him my school ID. I paid a couple of bucks and he gave me a little, round, yellow metal button with a fancy *M* on it. And I remembered how Isaac had collected these buttons—from the Met and the Brooklyn Museum and Natural History and places we'd go to on vacation. He had a whole bag of them in different colors. He just liked the way they all looked together.

The Egyptian rooms are off to the right of the lobby; most people head straight there, and I did too. I had to wait in line to walk through the exhibit, it was that packed. I got a little creeped out where the space gets real narrow like you're going through some underground tunnel. You really feel like you're walking into a tomb. I mean, the Egyptians' whole deal was about death. Or the death stuff is most of what was left of them and was put in the museums. Making bodies into mummies. Burying things that might come in handy when you're hanging around in the afterlife—sort of like that Chinese emperor did with his clay soldiers.

I don't know what I believe about all that. Heaven. Hell. The soul. Reincarnation. I want to believe there is a place where I'll see Isaac again. Maybe we all think something like that—need to—even if we say we don't.

Surrounded by all that death, I started to get that feeling like I couldn't breathe. Kind of like what I think people mean by a panic attack. I had to get away from all the mummies and other dead things and out of that crowded space. I left the exhibit as fast as I could move through all the people and got back out to the lobby. I stood there for a minute not sure what to do and then headed for the long, inside staircase and started to climb up. Right at the top was a sign pointing to the Asian collection. I walked in the direction of the arrow down a long hallway lined with vases in different shapes and sizes and amazing colors—bright blue, a deep green, and a dark, dark red.

I went into some rooms with really old pots—the cards next to them showed all these dates marked BCE. That stands for Before the Common Era. I thought about what that meant. Everything now, here in the good old CE, is nothing special? We're just common, everyday folks living in ordinary times? Or maybe it's that we all have something in common.

The next room was big and light and had high ceilings. Tall statues were all around. They looked a little like the Buddha guy Mom had given me, but blown up giant-size. They all seemed so peaceful. Their eyes were closed, like they were thinking about something inside them, not looking out at the world. I know it's weird, kind of New Age-y or spiritual or something, but for a minute they took away some of the strange feelings I was having. The signs said they were *bodhisattvas*—a word I'd never heard before. Later Orbach told me about them.

There were a few statues of a woman—a goddess— named Kwan Yin. She was posed in different ways, with flowers or animals or kids, but the best was a really outrageous one where she had a million arms sticking out. And I remembered when I'd seen something just like that that crazy time with Kim.

I left the room and found an indoor garden. I had to walk through this round door to get inside. A *moon gate*, the sign said. It wasn't a usual kind of garden—just some big rocks, a little pond, a few benches. I sat on one and watched the other people. It was eerie: I felt almost like I was waiting for someone. I saw this older lady and I thought she looked just like Lil. I mean, I thought for a second she *was* Lil. I closed my eyes and took some deep breaths because I was feeling sort of like I was floating away from myself.

Suddenly I heard someone saying, "You all right, son?" It was one of the guards. That sent me right back into real life. I was super embarrassed. I left the garden, went back through all the rooms, and down the staircase. On the main floor, before I made my way out of the museum, I stopped in the gift shop and looked at the postcards for a while. I bought one of Kwan Yin sitting on a lion. I know there are pictures on the Net, but I wanted to have one in my hand. A souvenir of something—I'm not sure what. I have it on my dresser at home next to the little Buddha. They keep each other company.

25

THE BALLOON IN THE CHIMNEY

So much was going on I began to actually look forward to my sessions with Orbach instead of dragging my ass there like I had always done before. I guess I was beginning to see that it was really helpful having a chance every week to try to put things together. To begin to figure out what was going on in my own head. I even set the alarm on my phone to make sure I'd be on time, so when Mom called down to me the next Saturday to hurry up, I was majorly annoyed.

"I am handling it," I yelled.

"I just don't want us to be late."

"You don't have to worry. And you don't need to come."

I knew she was hurt, but really. I was almost fifteen years old. I went to school on my own. I went to

Manhattan alone. So why did I still need my mommy to take me the few blocks to my shrink's?

I walked out by myself. A beautiful day. It was getting warmer and a lot of other people were on the streets. There were couples coming back from the farmers' market by the library carrying bags of vegetables and flowers, a few joggers heading up to the park, lots of parents pushing strollers. Ahead of me on the sidewalk was a mom with her little girl, maybe five or six, and she was teaching her to ride a bike without training wheels, making a big fuss every time the kid went a couple of feet. It was sweet.

When I got in to see Orbach there was so much I was thinking about it was hard to begin. I finally came out with something ridiculous like, "Ever been to China?"

Orbach just raised his eyebrows. I guess the question didn't seem totally out of the blue because Mom and Dad must have filled him in on things. He asked me to tell him, in my own words, about the adoption, the baby. He didn't say too much, as usual, just made some comment about how I seemed upset. Duh.

"I feel like I'm back in some alternate reality," I said, "like I was right after Isaac died."

"Can you talk more about that?"

I searched my brain for a way to explain it. "It's stupid, but you know those puzzles from the kids' magazine? *Highlights* or whatever? Where you're supposed to find the things that don't belong? Like there's a banana on the apple tree, a monkey wearing a tie? Or instead of smoke coming out of a chimney there's a balloon? I feel like I'm in the middle of one of those. We lose Isaac—a white, eleven-year-old boy, our flesh and blood. So we go get some baby Chinese girl we never heard about before?

"Nothing made sense after Isaac died. And then things started to calm down, and now this. I mean, I always heard you can go crazy from grief. Now I know what that means."

"Do *you* feel crazy?" he asked me.

I told him it was kind of a wild feeling. Like I had to keep moving. That was what made me run away to Manhattan.

"What's in Manhattan?"

I had already spilled it all to Sam, so it was easier telling Orbach. I had talked to him about Kim that once, after the first time we met, but he had no idea I had never stopped thinking about her, that I had gone off to look for her. And then taken Ecstasy with her. The good doctor pressed me on why the hell I did it.

"I don't know. It's like I need to forget everything. Pretend it's not happening. Before, it was the sadness, the explaining to people. But mostly now it's my parents. I don't understand what they're doing. How can they be thinking about a new house? A new kid? It's bullshit!"

"It's a lot to deal with."

"First we lost Isaac and became those poor Saturns. And now we're going to be the weirdo family with the Chinese kid. I just want things to be normal again."

"Aaron, my job is to help you get used to the new normal."

I wasn't ready to hear that. "It's too much work. I just want to get the hell away from all of it."

"You mean run away? And live like Kim?"

When Orbach said it, I realized how lame it sounded.

"No. I mean, before I met her, maybe I had some idea I could do it. Go away. Live on my own. A new life as somebody else."

"And how would that feel?"

"Quiet. Calm. Like before."

"So we need to get you to feel that way without doing something dangerous."

I knew I had made an asshole move. Taking some pill when I wasn't even sure what it was. Orbach didn't have to spell it out.

"You have to understand," he told me, "that if I ever suspect you're taking drugs again—if I even think you might be *thinking* about doing it again—I'd have to tell your parents."

"I know, I know. Don't worry. I'm not about to live on the streets. I don't want to become a druggie. You can't believe how awful it is for her. I didn't know how bad it could be. I feel like such a dick just leaving her there like that."

Orbach sighed. "I wish I could tell you there was an easy solution for someone like her. But we can't always save people."

But I realized I hadn't even tried to help her. What kind of schmuck was I? I got it in my head I had to at least try. Do *something* for her.

I thought about giving Kim money, or maybe talking her into finding her family, but I didn't have much to give her, and I was pretty sure there was no way she was going back to her parents. And then, suddenly, the solution became obvious: I would ask Kim to come home with me. That was the least I could do. She was in trouble. No one else seemed to give a shit. There was, I admit, another part of my thinking: *Mom and Dad are planning to fill the house with someone else. Some stranger. Fine. Let's see how they deal with it.*

26

PRETTY

By then I knew the places where I might find Kim. It was just a question of getting her alone without Lee or Hawk. Those guys scared me, and I hated them so much for how they were using her I didn't ever want to see them again.

I went some days after school and on weekends; whenever I had a chance, I'd hunt for her. It took about ten tries of traveling to the East Village and hanging around the streets before I saw her. One afternoon there she was, sitting on the steps in front of St. Mark's Church. Her feet were stuck out on the sidewalk. The rubber tips of her Keds, which must have been white once, were now a kind of yellow-gray. She was eating something from a plastic container, the kind they give out at the deli, and I had the thought that maybe she had fished it out of the garbage. When she looked up and saw me, she actually seemed happy.

"Hey, Aaron. See? I remembered your name this time."

"Yeah, well, I knew my charisma would win you over sooner or later."

I didn't think she got my joke, but I sat down next to her and stretched out my legs too, making people step around us. I didn't waste time, but right away told her my idea. I didn't want to wait and take the chance either of the evil duo would show up.

"Kim, what would you say to coming home with me? I mean, to live."

"What do you mean? Like live at your place?"

"Uh-huh."

"Where's that"?

"Brooklyn."

"Brooklyn? I never been."

"It's nice."

"What the fuck I'm gonna do in Brooklyn?"

"You'll stay with us, my family. You can go to school."

"Hah. I don't think so."

"Why not?"

"I hate fuckin' school. It's like they're in their own little world and they're always changing the rules and they treat you like shit."

"Well, let's not think about that yet. Just come."

"Who else'll be there?"

"My parents."

"And they're cool with it?"

"They will be. I don't always get along with them, but it'll be okay," I assured her with as much conviction as I could muster.

Maybe she heard the doubt in my voice. "People can let you down," she said. "People you thought you could trust. All the time."

Well, she was right about that. But I told her, "Not my mom and dad. They're not like your parents."

She suddenly was really angry. "You don't know nothing about my parents."

"I just thought—"

"Yeah, well, they got their own shit to deal with."

"Sorry."

"And, anyways, I can take care of myself."

I looked at her dirty clothes, bad teeth, unwashed hair, but didn't say anything.

Kim put the container down and wiped her hands on her jeans. She didn't seem annoyed anymore.

"So what's your answer?"

"I don't know," she said. "You rich?"

"No. I don't think so."

"You got a house?"

"Yeah."

"Well then."

I thought about that. I did have a house—two houses, actually. To Kim, it might have seemed I was friggin' Mike Bloomberg.

"Maybe I could go. For a little while."

"Great, great." All she had with her was some kind of droopy cloth bag, so I asked, "You need to get your stuff? Tell someone?"

She didn't respond, just looked at me in that way she had of making me think I had just said the dumbest thing in the world. Then she stood up and started walking.

At the Broadway-Lafayette stop I swiped her in with my MetroCard. People on the train were staring at her—and this is on the subway where you see all kinds of nut jobs. But I shook it off. I mean, that was the whole point—she was in bad shape.

It felt unreal being in my neighborhood with Kim, like two parts of my life that were so separate had slammed into each other. I had some lame idea that Kim would be examining everything and making little comments, like she'd find my neighborhood so fascinating or something, but she just walked with her head down and didn't talk at all. So I started pointing things out to her.

"There's the bagel store, and the comic book store, and over there is Pino's. They have the best pizza." I sounded like some demented tour guide.

When we reached my house she looked up and shook her head.

"Three floors you got? All three floors? I never knew no one had a house like this. Like a building or something. Like you got a whole building."

I let us in downstairs and told Kim to wait in my room while I went up to tell Mom and Dad she was there. She nodded and went over to my dresser where little Buddha guy was. "I know *him*," she said, picking up the figure and smiling.

My parents were surprised I was back so early. Those days they had gotten used to my disappearing for hours at a time. They were in the kitchen. I walked into the room and suddenly realized I had no idea what I was going to say. I know now I handled it badly, but maybe there was no way it would have worked out better.

"Hey, A-Team," Dad greeted me, a big smile on his face. He put on a British accent. "The old folks were just having a spot of tea. Would you care for a cuppa?" He was obviously happy I was home.

"No, thanks."

I can never keep anything from Mom. She saw right off that I was uneasy about something. "So what's up?"

"Uh, I brought a friend home."

"And?"

"She's a new friend."

"Your girlfriend?" Dad asked, sort of teasing me.

"No. No. This is someone I just met a few times."

Something wasn't adding up for them. "And why is she here, Aaron?" Dad asked, all the joking gone from his voice.

"She needs a place to stay. I mean, she needs a lot more than that. She's sort of homeless. Living on the street."

Mom and Dad both put down the mugs they had been drinking from. I could see them straining to understand, trying to figure out a reaction.

"Doesn't she have any family?" Mom asked after a moment.

"Maybe. It's not clear. But she doesn't want to be with them. Or can't."

"I mean, honey, if she's a minor ... how old is she?"

"I think my age."

"We have no right. No legal right."

"But she's in trouble. I want to help her."

"You said you just met her." Dad was suspicious.

"I saw her a couple of times before. In the City. What does it matter?"

"How can you even ask that?" Dad practically yelled at me.

Mom signaled for him to let it go. "Where is she?"

"In my room."

"Ask her to come up," she told me.

I don't know who was more nervous—me, Kim, or my parents. When Kim walked into the kitchen, I could see Mom was pretty shocked at what she looked like. But Mom recovered herself and starting asking Kim about her life and offering her food. And then she not so gently suggested she take a shower.

"I can wash your clothes for you too." The way she said it, it was like what she really wanted to do was burn her clothes for her.

"I got nothing else. You don't want me to be naked, right?"

I think that was Kim's attempt at humor. No one laughed.

Mom said to wait a second and went up to her room. Dad was yammering on about who knows what to cover the silence until Mom came back carrying a dress on a hanger.

"You can wear this," she told Kim, holding the dress out to her. "My things would be too big on you. But this was my cousin's. She was, uh, small, like you. I don't know why I saved it, really. She'd be happy to know someone got use out of it."

Kim went upstairs to use Mom and Dad's bathroom. Then Mom turned to me and let me have it.

"My God, Aaron. She's skin and bones. I'm not sure we can begin to help her. You're asking a lot of us. And for a complete stranger."

I was really snotty. "I thought that's what we did—bring strangers home."

"Aaron!" Dad snapped.

"What? What's the matter?" I came back at him. "She's not little and cute? Well, she's right here. I didn't have to go all the way to China to find her."

Mom grabbed the cups and spoons from the table and went to the sink to rinse them out. With her back to me she said in a very tired voice, "Does it make us bad people because we know our limits? You're right to think we don't want her here. It's too, well, just too complicated."

"So you're going to do nothing? That's such bullshit!"

Mom faced me. "I didn't say do nothing! Let me think a minute. Maybe we can find a safe place for her. That's something. But not here. We can't monitor her 24/7. And that's what she needs."

"She just needs to eat more and clean up and get back to school."

"Aaron, that's a lot. Think about it. When someone isn't eating, and isn't keeping themselves clean, and a kid your age isn't in school—those are signs of very big problems."

"Once she gets used to things here—"

Dad had had it. "And what about the drugs?"

I turned red. "What drugs?" I asked, as if I didn't know.

"Do you think we're stupid? Look at her! You think we can't tell? We live in the world too, Aaron, even if we're middle-aged."

I couldn't answer him because the lie stuck in my throat.

Mom spoke next. "You think we're full of shit because we won't take her on. That on the one hand we want to go halfway around the world to help some baby, but we won't help someone right in front of our eyes because it's too hard. But we're not adopting a baby to do good. We need this baby. We're not pretending we're saving the world."

"I didn't say—"

"It's what you meant," Dad interrupted.

Mom looked at me hard. "Just listen. She can stay for now, maybe a day or two. And then we have to find a place, a shelter, that's set up for kids like her. With experienced people to help them. I think we can get her to one of those."

"Maybe, if she wants to," I agreed reluctantly.

Dad exploded. "What are we talking about here? I'm not comfortable with her being here at all. We don't know this girl. We don't know what she'll bring into our lives if we get involved."

Mom dried her hands and went over to Dad. "Barry, it's for a short time. I'll make some calls and find a placement for her."

Dad walked away, clearly pissed. But he didn't say anything more and even made up the couch in the small room he used as a study.

Kim came downstairs in Lil's clothes. Lil was small like Mom said, but the dress was still way too big for Kim. She looked better—her hair was washed at least—but she looked even thinner and more lost. It made me think of when the kids at Mom's school went to the dress-up corner. Except they were having a good time putting on big clothes or fancy costumes, imagining themselves as moms and dads or firefighters and princesses. Kim definitely did not look like she was having fun.

It seemed a good idea to get her away from my parents for a while, so I suggested we go out for a walk. I didn't know whether I was hoping I'd run into somebody I knew, or hoping I wouldn't. I wasn't sure what to do, except maybe head over to the Tea Lounge where you can find a corner, sink into a couch and stay for a while. This time, as we walked, Kim was looking around at the stores and churches and people we passed on Seventh Avenue.

"This is just like Manhattan. Maybe cleaner," she remarked. "I thought it would be all different." She sounded a little disappointed.

"Well, if you want different, let's go up to the park."

"What's so chill about a park?" I realized she was thinking about the small one in Tompkins Square.

"You know. Like Central Park? The big one?"

"I heard of it," she snapped at me, annoyed. But I guessed she had never been there. Never even done that.

"This is a really beautiful park," I told her, back in tour guide mode. "Prospect Park." I started to reel off all the stuff Dad had told me, like about how the same famous guys who had designed Central Park had also designed Prospect Park, but I could tell she wasn't interested.

We went in through the Grand Army Plaza entrance and followed a cobblestone path that was lined with trees until we came out into the open. The Long Meadow was stretching out in front of us. Kim stopped and stared.

"This is fuckin' huge!"

People were lying on the grass; others were kicking soccer balls around. A couple of kids were even flying kites. It all looked so perfect. Like a story book. Like there was no trouble in the world.

We crossed the Meadow, passed the baseball fields, and stopped for a while in the Boathouse and looked out at the lake. Kim actually seemed to be enjoying it.

"You know what this is?" she said, talking more to herself than to me. "Pretty."

By the time we got back, Mom had supper ready. I noticed Kim didn't eat much. It made perfect sense that she was so thin. Mom and Dad exchanged looks.

After the meal, I took Kim back down to my room, and I asked if she'd like to play the Wii.

She said she'd done it before. "Hawk has it and let me use it one time. After I did something for him, you know? I could do you too."

"No, no," I said quickly. We tried playing for a while, but she made me so uncomfortable I told her I was tired and maybe she should go up to the study. She shrugged and left. I was beginning to think this wasn't such a good plan.

I fell asleep in my clothes and woke up around three in the morning and went upstairs to get something to drink. There was a noise in the hallway, and, forgetting in my half-awake state about Kim, I expected to see Mom or Dad walk into the kitchen the next moment. But, instead, I heard footsteps going up the stairs—slowly, as if someone was trying not to make noise. I didn't go to check. I thought maybe Kim had gone out in the middle of the night, and, to be honest, I didn't want to know why.

In the morning, she was gone, along with some of Mom's jewelry and all the money from the tin under my bed.

27

AND THE WINNER IS . . .

I felt kind of empty after that. Mom and Dad were good about it, not giving me a hard time. And Mom went ahead anyway and got the name of a place that would take Kim—if Kim would go. A big if. My parents were worried about my going back to the East Village to find her again and give her the information. They wanted to come with me, but I was afraid they might figure out about me and the drugs. That's a secret I've kept. Is it wrong? Am I kidding myself that they don't know? Maybe one day, when it won't upset them as much, I can tell them.

I put off going. I needed a bit of a break from the whole Kim thing. I felt dumb and hurt and tired.

I had been so caught up with Kim that I hadn't even spoken to Emma for a while. I wanted to talk to her.

Why? Because I missed her? Yes. But that was just part of it. It was mostly because I hoped she would make me feel better. I guess that was really selfish. Guess? I know it was. I was finally someone's boyfriend, and I was doing a sucky job at it.

When I did reach her, she sounded down. I figured it was because I hadn't called her. But that wasn't it. She had her own worries, which I had put out of my mind. Her father is an eleven out of ten on the douche scale, always leaning on her to get better grades in addition to practicing her instrument and joining the soccer travel team and keeping up with her dance lessons. She told me once, "I think he has a vision of me performing open heart surgery with one hand, playing the flute with the other, and standing en pointe while I'm doing it." At least she had kept her sense of humor about it. But forget about telling him she had a boo.

One night, after we'd been talking again, I was in my room actually trying to conjugate some French verbs for homework, when she called my cell. She seemed more upset than usual and wasn't saying much.

I wanted to know what was up. "What's going on? Did something happen?"

"Oh. Same old same old." I could hear in her voice that she'd been crying.

"Emma. I mean, you don't have to tell me, but if you want to, I'm listening."

"Well," she began, "I think this is it. The end. I think my parents are going to get a divorce."

I started to say I was sorry, but she cut me off. "No. I'm glad. My dad is just, well, awful."

"You always said he was."

"Yeah. But this time it was different." She started to cry again. "He hit my mom."

I was beyond angry. "Are you kidding me? The stupid bastard." Then I had an even worse thought. "He didn't hit you, did he?"

"No. No. Just Mom. Once. But hard. Really hard."

"Tell me."

She could barely talk. She was doing that hiccupping thing between every other word.

"He—he got laid off. And he went out and got—got drunk. And came home and—and just let Mom have it. For no reason."

"Is your mom okay?"

"Yeah. I mean—she's—furious. And so—so—unhappy. But she's—done with him. At least—at least he apologized. And left the house. And now I don't—know what's—going to happen."

I said everything I could to calm her down. About how it would work out and she and her mom would be happier. She stopped crying.

"Would it help," I asked, "if I came over or something?"

"That would be so great."

I went up to let Mom and Dad know where I was going. I think they were a little confused. Not one, but two girls now?

"This is Emma, the one I got the present for."

"It's a school night," Mom pointed out.

"She's having some family problems. I told her I'd be there. It's just over in Cobble Hill."

Mom kicked it to Dad. "Barry," she said, "what do you think?"

169

Dad made up his mind quickly. "Just be home by ten thirty," he told me.

I left the house and walked to the station. I took the F train to Emma's neighborhood, near school. It's a kind of fancy area, with some houses that were built way over one hundred years ago. Emma lived on a tiny street on one side of a small park in a red-brick carriage house, the kind of place that used to be for a horse and buggy back in the day and now only rich people could afford. Dad would go nutso for it. From the outside, it looked like some beautiful, peaceful, old-timey place. But some really bad shit had gone down inside.

I know it sounds harsh, but the whole thing with Emma's father helped me. I mean, for one, it made me realize that everybody has trouble in their lives. It gave me this idea for a reality show: I'd call it "Bad Parents," where people compete to see who's the worst at raising kids. It wouldn't be hard to find contestants. Hallie's father would have a good shot at winning. Not to mention Emma's dad and Owen's mom, of course. And the ones to beat—Kim's father and mother.

28

BEST RATE

As for my parental units, I could see that Mom was definitely on the upswing. I wasn't quite sure how I felt about that. I mean, it was good she was happier, but I still was pissed about the adoption. Mom had even started going to see me play baseball again. I was glad about that, until the day she brought An Rui along. It was a weekend when they were laying new concrete in the schoolyard, so the flea market wasn't on.

By now she and Mom were pretty tight and all, but I hadn't expected to see her show up at a game. And I hadn't told anyone on the team about China, so I was a little worried that maybe I'd have to say something. But then I realized that none of the guys thought An Rui had anything to do with me. In their minds, because they both looked Asian, she was connected to Sean.

So some of them used it as an excuse to make brilliant comments like, "Hey, Sean. That your real mom?" Everyone thought that was just HI-sterical. I mean, they call themselves his friends.

"Fuck you," Sean said.

It just got worse. "Hey, maybe she came to take you back to Japan," someone said.

"Korea," another boy corrected him.

"Whatever. Like it matters, idiot," the first kid shot back. "*Oh my little baby,*" he went on in a high voice. "*How could I know you'd grow up to be such a wonderful, handsome young man?*"

That brought another well-earned and louder "Fuck you!" from Sean. He stood up and left the dugout.

The guys were falling all over themselves laughing. Like I said, I always thought Sean was kind of a dick, but I couldn't go along with this. I told them all to quit it. One of them asked me, really nasty, "What's it to you, Saturn?"

Suddenly I was in the middle of a fight I hadn't started. But it was still my fight. I mean, would I have given a shit if it hadn't been for what was going on in my family? Would I have even thought the other kids were doing anything so terrible? But I did care, and I did know it was wrong. And I got scared that this kind of thing would keep happening if I had a Chinese sister. Dumb remarks, like the ones printed in that book of Mom's I had looked at. People telling her she spoke English really well when she came here as a baby and never spoke anything *but* English. Having to stand up for her and comfort her. And that, for some people, she'd always be different, always be That Adopted Chinese Girl.

I went over to Sean, even though we'd barely said two words to each other since the day I hit him.

"Hey. I'm sorry they're going after you. But they won't listen to me."

He shook his head. "I don't need you to defend me."

"I'm not defending anybody," I told him. "It's just that those guys are assholes."

"You just figured that out?"

That made me laugh. I hadn't known the guy could be funny. I apologized for the fight I'd had with him. He said it was NBD.

"Is it okay if I ask you about something?"

He knew exactly what it was. "Do you mean what's it like being adopted? Being an Asian with white parents?"

I nodded. Clearly Mom had already talked to his mom about our maybe-baby.

"I guess what just happened gives you some idea," he said.

"So people are always doing this kind of thing?"

"Not *all* the time. But enough. Whenever a chance comes up. And believe me, people find opportunities. Like when in school they decide it's time to 'celebrate our differences.' Me and the black and Hispanic kids are the differences."

I have heard that "celebrate" business a million times. I never thought about the fact that what it really means is what's different is anyone who isn't white.

"Of course," Sean added, "Koreans give me shit too."

"Why?"

"For not being Korean enough. Korean Pride or something. Like my parents take me to these Korean get-togethers. Kimchi fests. And most of the people are nice and all, but some of them to my face call me a banana or Twinkie—yellow on the outside, white on the inside—because I don't speak Korean or whatever."

Then I asked, "Do you ever think about your real parents back in Korea?"

Sean right away let me know my choice of words was a mistake.

"You see those two round-eyes over there?" he said, pointing to his mother and father. "They *are* my real parents. You mean my birth parents, tummy mommy. You'll have to learn the language."

"Tummy mommy?"

We both kept saying it and cracking up.

When I could catch my breath I told him, "Well, the adoption isn't definite."

Sean gave me one of those "yeah, right, believe that if you want to" looks. "You know, if, like, it ever comes up, your sister, when she's older, I could talk to her if she had any trouble or anything."

That really surprised me. I mean, that was going out of his way.

"Are you, like, angry at your, uh, birth mother for giving you up?"

He shrugged. "What can I say? I never knew her. I have to figure she had a reason, like being a single mom, which is not a cool thing to be over there, or having no money. So if she'd kept me, probably my life would've pretty much sucked. But, yeah, sometimes it gets to me and I really lose it. Maybe you noticed?"

We had to stop talking then because Larry was yelling at me that I was on deck. I took some practice swings. I could see Dad, Mom, and An Rui all looking my way. The guy ahead of me got a single. I walked to the plate and waited for the first pitch. And I had the weirdest feeling. That I could hear Isaac's voice cheering me on. And I hit the ball solidly, all the way into the outfield. I started running. And I kept on going even after the runner ahead of me was safe at home and Larry was signaling me to hold at third. I made it, but it was close. I was lucky. Larry gave me some grief about showboating, and I said I was sorry, but I had needed to score that run.

An Rui came up to me after the game and told me she thought baseball was *hen you yisi*—very much interesting. And that I was *zui hao*—best rate.

I had to laugh; it was so funny the way she said that. I hoped she didn't think I was making fun of her.

She asked me about the little bottle I'd bought from her. "Your *peng you*, your friend, she like it?"

"Yes. Thanks."

"Good. You will see at my country, *Zhong Guo*, many pretty things to buy."

"Well, it's not a sure thing about our going, and even if it was, Mom still has a lot to do to prepare things. So maybe it won't even happen and certainly not for a while."

I guess I spoke too quickly because she looked confused and told me, "*Bu ming bai*. I not clear."

I told her I wasn't either.

29

JUST A KID

One thing I *was* clear about: I had taken responsibility for Kim, and I couldn't put off looking for her any longer. So, once again, I was on patrol, trying to spot Kim on the streets of the East Village. I have such a mixed feeling about the place. On the one hand, I love the scene—the punk kids and old hippies, college students with their messenger bags, and artists lugging huge portfolios. But I know it's also filled with sad cases like Kim, and the cruelty of Hawk and his crew.

As a switch from pizza, I bought lunch to go from Benny's Burritos on Avenue A. I crossed over to Tompkins Square Park and sat on a bench near the playground to eat. I was looking at the children run around with their parents following after them. Some of the kids were really small, just starting to walk, and they moved all stiff like little baby robots. And then I spotted a girl I was sure was Kim standing near the swings with a couple of guys. One was definitely Lee. He and the other man were holding brown paper bags, and I guessed there were liquor bottles or cans of beer inside because every once in a while they raised the bags to their lips and took a sip.

I wrapped up my half-eaten food and walked over, stopping outside the fence to watch the three of them. I looked at the girl. She was bent over and swaying a little. She looked like she was moving in slo-mo. And it didn't take a genius to figure out she was on something heavy-duty.

I took a deep breath and forced myself to walk towards them, past the sandbox and climbing equipment and all the kids and people and strollers. When he saw me approach, Lee made a move like he was going to stop me, but then he lowered his arm and gave me a weird smile. When I was right next to them, I leaned down and said, "Kim, Kim" a few times before the girl looked up at me. And when she finally did, I saw it wasn't Kim.

Lee stepped in between us and told me to leave her alone.

"Who's this?" I yelled at him. "Where's Kim?"

"Get the fuck away."

"I'm a friend of Kim's," I told him. "Tell me where she is. I need to talk to her."

Lee mimicked me. "Oh, I need to talk to her. It's something that's so fuckin' important." He laughed in a really nasty way. "You are one dumbass kid and you don't have no business here."

He was at least ten years older than me, six inches taller, and forty pounds heavier, but I was so pissed I didn't care. I shouted back, "*She's* just a kid. What business do *you* have with her? Or this girl? You bastard!"

He just shook his head. "You don't know what you're dealing with, guy. Hey, I'm doing you a favor."

I kept looking at the girl, hoping she'd give me some kind of sign that she understood what was happening and would move away from him. But all she did was reach out kind of shaky and put her hand on Lee's shoulder. He slipped his arm around her waist. I stood there like an idiot and kept saying things to her like, "I can help you, there's a place you can go," but even as the words came out of my mouth I knew it was pointless.

I thought about looking for a cop, but the three of them would be long gone by the time I found one. And then what would I even say? And what if Hawk came after me? Went after my parents? So I didn't even resist when Lee pushed past me, leading the girl out of the park. I just stayed there like a fool, like I was stuck in the ground, watching them go.

Then I realized I had been holding on to my unfinished burrito the whole time. Just perfect. It was starting to leak through the aluminum foil. I threw it in the nearest garbage can and headed out of the park. I was disgusted with myself, almost crying. I wandered the streets for hours after that, trying to find Kim, desperate to make things right, and pretty certain I had no chance of succeeding. I was totally, completely powerless. This was way worse than that time I couldn't cheer up Owen. I knew it was hopeless. Kim was already lost. And that there was another girl being abused, and there'd be another one after that.

An Rui had said I was *best rate*. Yeah. I was best rate all right. A best-rate loser.

30

A LOSE-LOSE SITUATION

That day really shook me up. The bad dreams started again. They had gradually tapered off after Isaac died, but now, like before, they came every night. I would see Isaac in the distance, standing a block or two away from me somewhere on St. Mark's Place. I mean, I knew it was Isaac even though I couldn't get a good look at him. I felt really happy to see him, but also that there was something strange about it, not quite right. I was frantic he was going to step out in the street and get hit by a car or something. So I tried to go over to him, but I couldn't. It was hard to move, that walking in quicksand thing that happens in dreams. I couldn't talk, either, to warn him; I kept thinking his name but nothing came out of my mouth. Then I saw Mom and Dad going past, and I tried and tried to call out to them that Isaac was there, but I couldn't do that either. And they just went by, missing the chance to see him. I couldn't believe how sad that was. Then I woke up, my heart pounding.

I made an appointment to see Orbach in the middle of the week, not wanting to wait until the next Saturday. I told him I felt like I was losing Isaac all over again. That that's what the dream was about.

"It sounds like it," Orbach agreed. "But there are some details in it that make me think maybe it's also about something in addition to that. Anything else it makes you think of?"

Of course it was also about Kim, and maybe even about Emma. I felt so bad because I hadn't saved Kim, hadn't helped the other girl, either. Couldn't do anything real to change Emma's situation. "I'm less than useless. I'm not doing anybody any good. I feel like a loser idiot asshole."

"Well, I love the rich description," he said, smiling. Sometimes old Orbach shows his sense of humor. "But I don't think it's entirely accurate. First of all, you tried to do something. You felt a responsibility."

"And did zip."

"You tried, Aaron."

Something else was bothering me. "What if I only wanted to try to help to make myself feel better? Like some weight would be off me. Like I can stop feeling guilty about Isaac. Maybe I don't really care about Kim or Emma. I say something nice or pull some stunt or whatever and then everyone thinks I'm this wonderful person and for about two minutes I'm okay. But then I start to feel I'm a selfish prick. I do things for the wrong reasons and don't accomplish anything anyway. A lose-lose situation."

Then Orbach asked me something I didn't expect—if I thought Isaac was a good person.

"Of course," I told him.

"And was he nice to people just to make himself feel better?"

Well, I saw where he was going with that. I remembered what Sam had said about me beating on myself. It's funny—sometimes when you're feeling bad you just look around for reasons to feel even worse.

Talking about Isaac made me think about the day I went to the museum. I started telling Orbach about the statues I saw, the ones who looked so peaceful. That's when he explained to me about bodhisattvas. The guy digs Asian stuff. He said the bodhisattvas look so calm because they have reached nirvana—a feeling that everything is chill. No more worries. And then they help other people to get there too. That's their job. Their purpose. Maybe, and I know this sounds cheesy, we can all be bodhisattvas in a small way. Maybe even me. Someday. It's not easy. Maybe wanting to try is the first step.

I'm still working on it.

31

SAVING THE WORLD

Things had cooled off at Emma's house since her father had moved out, and I could tell how much happier she was. I mean, she's got a good heart; it's not easy for her to have such a bad relationship with her father, but it was clearly a plus he wasn't around so much.

I wanted to stay close to her, so I knew I had to tell her everything. First, about Kim. I asked her to go with me after school to "our" bench on the Promenade. We sat looking out at the Bridge and the skyline as I confessed my little Ecstasy escapade. Emma took my hand and said she was worried, even when I promised her it was a one-off. And then she told me she was hurt that I hadn't shared something so important with her. And that that something involved another girl.

She asked, looking down at the cobblestones, "Did you, uh, like her?"

"It wasn't about that," I said. And I think that's true. I mean, if anything, I found Kim the opposite of attractive. "She just kind of appeared in my life. I never even thought about how I felt about her. It's like, in a way, I needed her. And then it was like I had to do something for her. Like I was trying to not feel so bad about not helping Isaac. Or, who knows, maybe I was trying to *be* Isaac. Isaac would've helped her."

"Maybe."

I got a little angry at that. I let go of her hand. "You didn't know him."

"Aaron, he was eleven years old."

I'm not sure why, but that actually made me cry. In front of her and all the people walking by. Not good. But it was like something had opened up, and then I told her in a rush about what had been going on with my parents and all about the adoption.

She waited until I settled down. Then she said, "This could be good, you know? And pretty exciting. Going to China? Getting a sister?" I think she was happy to have something to think about, other than her father.

It was weird—I realized that when I was talking to Emma about it, I didn't make the whole baby thing sound so awful. Was I getting used to the idea? Not that I was exactly enthusiastic. Emma picked up that I was kind of mixed about it.

"I'm not an expert here," she said. "I'm an only child from a seriously messed up family. This is huge. And it seems to me that it's okay to have doubts about it."

Man, was I grateful for that.

Her reaction was a whole lot calmer than Olivia and Meredith's. It was almost the end of the school year, and the five of us—me, Sam, and the three girls—were sitting, as usual, in a Starbucks. When I told them the news, Olivia and Meredith went berserk, like they were the ones getting a baby sister.

"Aaron! This is unbelievable! This is the definition of awesome!" Olivia cried.

They started talking about how cute all those little Chinese girls were that they saw around the neighborhood and who they knew who was adopted. Sam kept using the word "heartwarming." I couldn't rein them in.

"How soon are you going?" Meredith asked.

I explained that the whole adoption deal was going to take awhile and be pretty expensive. "Plus we have a ton of stuff to do beforehand. Like we're planning to move over to Lil's house—my mom's cousin's old house. And me and my mom and dad will have to be working all summer."

I already knew Emma wasn't going to be around for July and August. Her mother was taking her to Europe. I was really sad I wouldn't be seeing her, but I figured she deserved something special like that. Thinking about Lil, I had told Emma to check out the art in Italy.

Olivia started complaining that her parents had signed her up for some kind of charity trip. "It's this thing where you go to a poor country and help build sewers or some such. Ugh."

Sam was actually impressed. "Wow. That sounds cool."

Meredith shook her head. "Oh, please. She's going to be with a bunch of other rich kids only doing it so they have something to put on their college apps."

Olivia defended herself. "It's not exactly going to be luxury accommodations. More like the best in slum living."

Meredith rolled her eyes. "You are such a snob! You should be happy you can afford to go. Not to mention these people have nothing, and you have a beautiful house and clean water and everything else you've ever wanted."

"Who are you to talk?" Olivia asked, really ticked off. "What the hell are you giving back to humanity? You're going off to some arts camp where you put on musicals. I mean, really. *Musicals?*" She turned to the rest of us. "What planet is *that?*"

It was starting to get ugly, but Sam stood and held out his arms to Meredith. "She will share her creative vision with the world. Not that that compares with building one good toilet, but still."

"Well, anyway," Meredith added, looking at me, "your family is taking care of all that humanitarian stuff for me. I mean, what a great thing—helping some poor little Chinese orphan."

I stopped her right there. "That's not why my parents want to do this. They're doing it for them."

"You make it sound like they're being selfish," Olivia said.

"I'm just being honest."

"Aaron, I know how you're feeling, but think about it. Just because in some ways you can see it as selfish doesn't mean it isn't also doing good," Emma said.

I guess it hit me that there was a different way to look at it. That maybe I'd been holding on to the wrong idea. Nothing was going to bring Isaac back. My parents weren't—aren't—bad people. Far from it. They needed to do this. They deserved to do this if it would give them even an atom's worth of happiness. Sitting there with a chai latte in my hand, I felt a lot of the anger just slip away.

32

ON BOARD

That summer I began to be aware of, more and more, all the Asian people in the neighborhood. Sean, of course, and An Rui. But also a couple of teachers at the school on Seventh Avenue, the neighbors up the block, the mailman, Lito, who's Filipino, the Korean couple that owns the corner grocery, and all the workers at the Japanese, Chinese, Thai and Vietnamese restaurants we go to. I guess I hadn't been paying attention to that sort of thing. I mean, it's good not to be hyper-aware of someone's race, but that doesn't mean you shouldn't realize there are different kinds of people in the world.

What was really strange, though, is that suddenly there seemed to be nothing *but* little Chinese girls all over the place. Tucked into strollers, running along the sidewalk, laughing on the swings in the playground.

They must have been there before, but they never appeared on my radar. Dark-haired kids with parents that didn't match. But the parents were doing all the stuff real parents do, like warning them to not bump into people on the street, or feeding them little pieces of bagel, or telling them they had to share their toys, or wiping melted ice cream off their faces. It made me think—maybe that's okay. Maybe families don't have to match. Take Sam, for example. He's over six feet and no one else in his family is that tall. And me and Isaac—everyone always said we didn't look like brothers. My hair is curly and light brown—nothing color—and my eyes dark brown, like Dad's. Isaac looked more like Mom. His hair was really dark and straight. His eyes were green. He was a cute kid.

Dad was busy getting Lil's house ready for us to move into, and Sam, to my surprise, turned out to be a big help. Never would have thought Sam would enjoy doing that stuff so much—learning about joists and soffits and like that—that he would drop the idea of film school, at least for then. I came over on weekends and they gave me the shit jobs like stripping wallpaper. But it was fun hanging with them.

Emma had left on her trip. We were talking back and forth on Skype. She looked and sounded good. She said she even had a chance to speak some French and realized how bad her accent was. But I was a little worried that she'd fall for some French guy. I guess I was also afraid she'd fall for some Italian guy. Or English guy. Pretty much I worried whichever country she was in.

I had a good time working at the Saturn School. When it was my birthday the kids each made me a crayon and construction paper card. And my man Owen came there for day camp. I'm not going to say he got normal all of a sudden, but he didn't need to be Velcroed to my side all the time. He actually played with other kids, and there was a whole lot less teasing.

One afternoon Owen was in the block corner building this amazing castle thing. I mean really elaborate, with a drawbridge and towers and a moat he made from plastic containers filled with water. And I see Justin the Cruel on his way over. My first instinct was to tackle him because I was convinced he was going to knock it all down. I mean, that's the sucky kind of thing he usually does. But that day he stopped and looked at what Owen had made—and then asked if he could help.

So there were definite high points, although I really missed Emma and went straight over to her house the minute I knew she was back.

I hadn't noticed the time I'd been there before how girly her room was—frilly curtains on the window, a pile of fancy pillows and stuffed animals on her bed. I guessed Mom would be buying things like that for the baby.

It was a little awkward seeing her that first time. Somehow we started talking, and then we started kissing, and it was pretty amazing. We didn't let it get too far—her mom was in the house. But I definitely got the idea of where it was leading.

Things were pretty chill between me and Mom and Dad, now that I wasn't stomping around furious at the world the whole time. Still, I was only half-paying attention to what was going on with the adoption; it was my way of dealing.

But I couldn't stay out of it when the woman from the social work agency was about to show up to do a home study to check us out. Mom had asked me over and over if I thought I could see her and not be too negative. I mean, up to then, I didn't have to really do anything about the adoption; I was just a bystander.

"Can I just be honest with her?" I said. "You can't want me to lie."

"No, of course not," Mom answered. "I want you to say exactly what you're feeling."

"Then I'll tell her that I want you guys to be happy. But that I'm not entirely sure if this is okay. That I still feel we're not doing right by Isaac." But I didn't say it like I had before, all mad at them.

Mom nodded. "Yes. Say that if you mean it. But is there nothing else, honey? Do you see anything positive now?"

I thought about that. How it would be nice to have a little kid in the house. We were people who liked kids. Hell, I even liked Owen, and he was no one's idea of cute and cuddly. And when Mom and Dad had decided to have a second kid, did it mean that they had stopped loving me? Of course not. So getting this baby wasn't going to mean we would stop loving Isaac.

I told Mom I was on board.

33

THESE PEOPLE

Just before school began again, Emma, Olivia and
Meredith and me and Sam got together to have lunch
in Chinatown. It was Sam's idea—he said it was a trial
run for my trip to China. Although, at that point, Mom
and Dad still didn't have a clue when we would actually
be going. But by then I knew I was looking forward to
it, a little.

We took the F to the East Broadway stop, and even
while still in the station it almost was like being in
another country. Mostly Asian people—and the five of
us. I felt we kind of stuck out. I remembered what Sean
had called his parents—round-eyes. We were practically
the only round-eyes there.

Chinatown is an old part of the city where the streets
are narrow and don't run in straight lines. Dad says it's

pre-grid. Before they laid out New York like a gigantic tic-tac-toe board. All those little winding streets were packed with people. I saw, right out on the sidewalk, a man fixing shoes and another at a table repairing watches, and guys offering to paint your name in fancy letters or Chinese characters on long sheets of paper. There were a million tiny shops with scarves, backpacks, and T-shirts hanging at the entrance, and tables piled with cheap jewelry. Every few feet was a market or stand selling fruits and vegetables or a seafood store with boxes set up outside full of smelly heaps of fish, shrimp, eels, even frogs, on ice.

Almost all the store signs were in Chinese. Some had English translations, which were too weird to believe. My all-time fave: "Five Brothers Fat Haircutting and Herbal Remedies Shop." But I liked it all. It was so different and so busy. I was in a good mood.

We were all starving, but passed up the restaurants that had shiny, red-colored cooked ducks dangling from metal hooks in the window because Emma refused to go in. We finally went to a place that was kind of plain and old-looking, with the linoleum on the floor peeling off. Olivia said it was gross. When we sat down she made some remark about how we should be careful what we order because "these people will eat anything, like cats and dogs."

That took away the good feeling, fast. I mean, my sister-to-be was one of "these people." I told her she shouldn't say things like that, and Emma shot her a look.

"Don't go all holier-than-thou on me," Olivia said back to us.

"But you're being ridiculous," Meredith told her. "Embarrassing, actually."

I was trying not to explode at Olivia, but I did tell her to get over herself.

"Girl, you're missing out on a whole big part of the world with that attitude," Sam chimed in. "And let's examine the hypothesis, shall we? Say you can go out and gather up these poor little stray animals. Free, but labor-intensive. Or maybe you buy them from someplace even, some creepy illegal supplier. Then you have to unload them at night. Hide them from the Department of Health. Bribe some people. I guess do the skinning yourself. Then make damn sure it looks like chicken after you prepare it. Wouldn't it be easier to just serve regular meat?"

Then Emma asked us why it was okay to eat any animal. "Why is eating an innocent cow or cute little lamb any better than eating a dog or cat?"

Well, she had a point. I guess everyone else thought so too, because we wound up ordering a whole lot of tofu.

Olivia wasn't totally ready to drop the argument, though. "Come on. You're going to tell me this, uh, eating establishment, isn't different from what you're used to?"

"Duh. I thought that was the whole point," Emma said.

"Well, can't different be awful?"

"But it's *not* awful," Emma said. "It's just not the usual kind of restaurant you go to."

Meredith, her mouth full of sesame noodles, pointed out that the food was delicious. "Maybe they just don't have the money to fix the place up. Maybe it's not important to them. Maybe it's like a sign of how much they care about the food that they don't even think about what the place looks like."

Sam was looking around. "Although I could do wonders with it."

I rolled my eyes. "Oh man, one summer fixing up a house and it's *Extreme Makeover: Home Edition!*"

We walked around some more after lunch so the girls could spend way too much time looking at pocketbooks and trying on slippers and playing with fans. Then we went into one of the bubble tea cafés, but the "bubbles" turned out to be sticky balls of something or other at the bottom of the cup, and we pretty much lost interest after a few sips. On the way out of the café, Emma asked me what I thought of Chinatown.

"It's my kind of place: intense."

"Although you seem a little less intense lately."

"I guess it's true. I feel, well, not exactly happier. Just less sad."

She nodded. "Me too. Now we both need to believe it's not so terrible to feel okay."

I squeezed her hand. I did feel better than I had in a while. But I was still worried about how things were going to turn out. "Being here makes me think about how the baby would be a part of a whole big something that I'm not, that Mom and Dad aren't, either."

She looked up and down Division Street, at all the stores and signs and restaurants and people. "But think of it this way," she said. "We're here now. So we are a part of this in a small way. And when you go to China, and then bring home your sister, you'll for sure be a part of it."

"You really think so?"

She nodded. We stood there grinning at each other like a couple of idiots. I was about to kiss her when the others stopped us—rolling their eyes, shaking their heads and laughing—and pulled us back toward the subway station.

34

SO WHAT HAPPENS NOW?

Just after Christmas, Mom's friend Grace Miller, the one who'd lost her son, had her baby. I was nervous—afraid Mom was going to start crying or something. But I didn't give her enough credit. I heard her on the phone with Grace, congratulating her. She said, "I only hope our two girls will be as good friends as we are."

It was good Mom had her own baby to look forward to. She had been working for months and months to get everything ready. It seemed that, on top of going through the home study, Mom and Dad were always running to government offices, filling out a million forms, putting together information on every last detail about our lives to give to the Chinese authorities. The whole adoption thing seemed to be taking forever. Plus, people asked us about it like every second. I mean, after

Isaac died, it was like people didn't know what the hell to say. Now they couldn't shut up.

It was almost the end of January when Mom yelled out from the kitchen, "I've finished the paperwork!" She had just gotten off the phone with the adoption agency. Dad and I rushed in, and it was group hug time.

Dad was really pumped, but he asked, "Are you sure, Claire? I mean, I know we got the accountant's statement and the fingerprints, but what about our marriage license? Did you ever get a copy of that?"

"Marriage license. Check," Mom told him as she took glasses down from the cabinet.

"What about the references?"

"Check." She put the glasses on the table.

Then Dad started to ask, "What about—" and I guess Mom thought she knew exactly what was coming because suddenly her face fell. She looked straight at him and said very calmly, "Everything, Barry."

It took me a second to realize what was going on. She thought he was talking about the death certificate. For Isaac. She even had to get a copy of that to show the Chinese officials.

Dad shook his head. "I just meant was everything notarized or whatever else we had to do."

Mom told him the adoption agency was going to take care of all that. No one said anything for a while. To break the silence I asked, "So what happens now?"

"We wait," Mom said. "For Beijing to assign us a child."

"How long?"

"I'm not entirely sure. A few months, I think. If everything goes okay."

"What do you mean? Why shouldn't everything go okay?" I had just taken it for granted that there weren't going to be any glitches from then on. The idea all of a sudden that maybe something would go wrong, that we wouldn't get the baby, made me go a little nutso.

Mom tried to calm me down, told me that there could be delays, maybe something would come up at the Chinese end that would put things on hold for a while, that she wasn't worried. "But it's out of our hands now."

It was so weird thinking that whether or not we got a baby—and if we did which baby—would be decided by some people in some office somewhere in Beijing.

Mom poured ginger ale into our glasses. She asked us to raise them in a toast.

"To new life," Dad said.

We all took a sip. We smiled at each other. And each one of us was happy. And also thinking about Isaac at the same moment.

35

NEW HAPPINESS

And then, as we waited, and were settling into Lil's house, another summer turned to autumn, and the call came from our agency that we had a child. They forwarded the letter from China. Attached to it was a tiny picture of a baby girl named Xin Yue. We were scheduled to pick her up in eight days. It was just about three years since we'd lost Isaac.

We went into overdrive. Dad put the finishing touches on the baby's room, and postponed all his jobs, Mom got a sub, I told my teachers I'd be missing two weeks of school. It was eerie—so much of it was like what we had to do after Isaac died.

We took turns carrying around the photograph. It showed a chubby little girl, around three months old, being propped up in a highchair by someone. You could just make out the hand behind her. Mom still has it in her wallet.

Sam and the girls met me at Pino's the night before our trip to say goodbye.

Emma was crying a little.

"I'll miss you. You better e-mail or Skype or at least tweet every day and tell me everything that's happening."

"Definitely."

Sam shook his head. "Don't be so sure. The Chinese government is always trying to shut down the Internet. And besides, you don't want to take valuable time away from shopping for my presents."

"Get me something too," Olivia demanded.

"Like you brought anyone presents from Costa Rica last summer," Meredith muttered.

"It was Guatemala. And there was nothing to buy!"

"Right."

"I'm not going to China to go shopping," I told them.

The girls gave each other a look. "I don't even know how to respond to that," Meredith said.

Olivia wanted to know if I was excited. I said I was. But also scared. What would the baby be like? What would our lives be like? Would I love her? Would she love me?

Meredith grabbed Xin Yue's picture out of my hand.

"You can't tell anything's wrong with her. Are you sure about that?"

"It's something with one of her arms. But they're already working on it over there. And Mom spoke to a doctor here who said it'll be fine."

"Well, she's seriously cute!"

I had to admit Meredith was right. Weird how attached I was to that picture.

"I hope they're doing right by her at the orphanage," Emma said, looking over Meredith's shoulder.

"Things aren't so bad in the Chinese orphanages now," Sam told her. "Especially with all the Western money coming in. Fixing things up, training nannies, foster parents."

Olivia stared at Sam. "Is there anything you don't know about?" she asked him.

Sam pretended to think for a moment. "Tough question. Off the top of my head—no. But I'll get back to you. I mean, truthfully—full disclosure—I am a little shaky on string theory."

Olivia shook her head. "Who invited *him?*"

"Don't mind her," Emma said. "We love you, Sam."

Sam turned bright red.

Meredith asked what the baby's name meant.

"We asked An Rui, you know, my mother's friend, and she said Xin Yue means New Happiness."

"Wow," Sam said. "That's heavy, dude."

"Do you think they deliberately gave you a baby with a name like that?" Olivia asked. "Otherwise, it's almost spooky."

"I don't know. I think they give all the girls 'good' names. Lucky names. A little something extra because of the tough start they had."

"I don't understand how someone could give away this little cutie," Meredith said.

I recited the short version of the one-child deal. When the girls heard about babies being left on the street, they were shocked.

"That's horrible!" Meredith cried.

"It wasn't quite that cold," I reassured them. "An Rui translated the documents we got with Xin Yue. They said she had been left at a police station when she was three days old."

"Uh, I repeat. That's pretty harsh," Meredith answered.

"I know that sounds bad. But whoever did it left her at a place where they knew there were people." I was just reciting the line we'd been given from the adoption agency, trying to make it seem not as sad as it was. I mean, it is true—at least she wasn't thrown in a dumpster or anything—but it's still kind of awful.

It can't have been easy for anyone to leave their kid. They must have believed the baby would be taken care of. They must have felt they had no choice, or someone forced them to do it. I know it broke their hearts. I can't stand to think about all the pain—ours, for losing Isaac, the Chinese parents for losing their kids. It's not the same, I know—the Chinese think their kids will have a shot at a good future—but they still must feel the emptiness every day. You don't ever get over something like that.

There are times when I imagine what it was like: a woman sneaking along the streets of a town, hugging a baby, tightly wrapped, looking to the left and right. Then she checks the address, carefully places the small package on a stone step, and quickly runs away, crying the whole time. She hides, waits until someone spots the baby, then sneaks off, head down. It was like a scene in a B movie. But it had really happened. It had happened to the little girl who was about to become my sister.

36

HI, LILY

And now I'm here on this bus, with all these strangers, in the People's Republic of Friggin' China, going from the airport to the hotel in Changsha. Not exactly one of your major tourist areas like Beijing or Shanghai. A place I never heard of before that's now part of my life.

I had an idea of what China would be like: a mash-up of Chinatown and the art I'd seen in the bookstore and stuff Orbach talked about. Cities that were all curvy streets with tiny eating places set in old buildings, and behind them mountains sprinkled with pagodas and temples where people were wearing long robes and drinking tea. *Right.* Already, what I see out the window is not at all what I expected. We're on this wide highway that's all lit up. And just now we passed a group of huge structures that I thought was the remains of an ancient town, but Jing Jing, our guide, said it's actually brand new, the world's largest restaurant, made to look like the Forbidden City where the emperors used to live. Sort of like if someone built a McDonald's that was an exact replica of the White House.

And, just because the biggest restaurant in the world wouldn't be enough to have out here, down the road is a gigantic water park. And wait, there's more. When we pull up to the hotel, we see a monster Ferris wheel right across the street from us. Really. It must be like thirty stories high. It's like something from Six Flags. Isaac would be old enough now to go on it.

We get off the bus and enter the hotel. It's all marble and glass and gold. There's a waterfall in the lobby. I think it's kind of cool, actually, but Mom mouths *tacky* to Dad. I don't think it was their idea of China, either. Mom says the place looks like a mall.

We stand around in the lobby talking to the other families who are also here adopting babies. Everybody seems nice enough; a few have their other kids with them. I feel like a weirdo because I'm the oldest kid here. I mean, they're pretty cute and all, but there's no one to hang with. Mom tells me I'll be a help after we get the babies—and the kids throw fits when it hits them that from now on they're going to have to fight for their parents' attention. Instant sibling rivalry.

None of us feels tired, even though we've been traveling for most of a day. We check in, then unpack and turn on the TV. BBC News is on. Another disconnect. I didn't expect to hear English.

In the morning, we wash quickly, and Mom reminds me to be careful to use the bottled water to brush my teeth. It doesn't fit—the Chinese can afford to build all this fancy new stuff, but you can't drink the water. It's like China is two places at once. I mean, it's kind of interesting, but it just doesn't add up. The same people busy making everything look modern passed some law like from the middle ages about how many kids you can have.

We meet the other families for breakfast in the hotel cafeteria. Dad is happy when he sees there's some coffee—until he tastes it. I guess that's why China is famous for its tea.

The place is filled with local people who have come in to eat. They keep staring at us. They obviously don't get too many Westerners here. It's a little freaky trying to have breakfast with a million eyes on you. And I realize this is what it feels like to be different, not to look like the rest of the people around you.

Mom and Dad need to meet with some official this morning before we all take the bus to the town where the orphanage is. I don't really want to tag along, would like a little time off from always being with my parents or a group. As we walk out of the hotel, I ask if I can look around the city while they go to their appointment. Mom looks worried.

"I'll be okay," I tell her. "I'm a New Yorker." I say it like a joke, but I can tell it makes Mom and Dad think about me being with Kim.

All Dad says is, "Just be careful."

Mom checks her watch. "I can't argue with you now," she says, obviously upset, but digs in her purse and hands me some *yuan*. "Take this in case you need something. And don't be too long. The bus leaves at nine thirty." She also gives me a card with the hotel's name and address on it in English and Chinese.

I head out. It's not raining, but the sky is gray from pollution. Just outside the hotel there's a high stone wall with little statues of lions or dogs dotting the top of it. It's something that actually looks like it's been around for more than two minutes, and I follow it for blocks. Maybe it was built a long time ago to keep the city safe from attackers. In front of it, people have set up little businesses—fixing shoes, frying pancakes and dumplings, selling odd metal parts. There's a guy who's sitting there poking in peoples' ears, cleaning them. It reminds me of stuff I saw in Chinatown, and I realize that some of the old China was transported directly to the streets of Manhattan.

The sidewalk ends at a construction site. I'm looking up at scaffolding made of nothing but sticks of wood. And guys way up walking on it. Dangerous, much? I don't think Dad would approve. I wonder how there can be so many new buildings if this is how they're doing it.

In the middle of a big intersection a traffic cop is standing on a little platform trying to direct a tangle of pedestrians, buses, cars, taxis, trucks, scooters, and bikes. I cross over to a crowded, wide street, lined with clothing stores and restaurants—even fast-food places. I notice that at one point the mass of people on the side-walk kind of parts in half, as if they don't want to step on something. And then I see what it is. A man is actually lying flat out on his stomach on the ground, a cup next to him. He raises one hand, palm up—begging. I never saw anything like that. Not even the homeless guys on the Lower East Side were in that bad a way. It makes me sadder than I've been in a while. I give him all the money I've got.

Farther down the block I see the entrance to a covered market, and I walk in. A few places are selling some kind of fish, all bloody, and there are skinned goats hanging from another stall. Lots of vegetables too, like cabbage, and fruit—melons and bananas. The place really smells, and it's so packed I can barely walk. And people are stopping in their tracks to look at me and saying things to me, and I can't understand a word. It's a little scary. Not being able to speak to people—I feel kind of helpless. And really stupid. I think maybe I should have waited to go with Mom, who, at least, knows a few words.

By now, I can tell I'm lost. So I kind of thrust the card from the hotel in the face of a woman in one of the market stalls, and, luckily, she gets what I'm asking. She nods and points and says something. I start walking the way she showed me and somehow find my way back. The bus is parked in front of the hotel next to a line of cars decorated with red and yellow paper flowers for a wedding. Behind them I can see Mom and Dad anxiously looking for me.

The bus heads off along the same road we were on the night before. There isn't too much traffic, but the driver uses his horn like crazy anyway. The sun might be out above all the smog, but it's hard to tell. As we get further from the city, we pass some rice fields with a couple of people in them in those pointy straw hats, and I even see an honest-to-God water buffalo. Mostly what we're passing, though, are these square, two-story houses made out of concrete that line the highway.

They're like the kind of houses the little kids at Mom's school draw—a door on the bottom and two windows on top. Dad makes a face at how ugly they are. But as we drive along I see one really cool thing. There's a steep hill with wooden steps attached to it and a little building on top that I guess is a shrine or some other religious thing, and people on the ground are walking from opposite directions toward the hill, meeting at the foot of the stairs, and then slowly, one after the other, climbing up.

One woman in our group has to pee really badly. Jing Jing tells the driver to stop, and she takes the woman into one of the concrete houses to ask to use the bathroom. The woman comes back and tells us that the people were very nice but that they had only a squat toilet—a hole in the floor. Jing Jing says we all better get used to it. The woman also says that the people had a pig inside the house, which we all think is HI-sterical. But Jing Jing explains that the word, the character, for home—*jia*—is the symbol for pig with a roof over it. I love it. I can't wait to tell Sam.

We get to the orphanage town, Yueyang, around noon. The place isn't much to look at, except for the part bordering the huge lake. Jing Jing shows us the famous tower, which really isn't much of a tower—maybe three floors—but it's actually old and really looks back-in-the-day Chinese with the ends of the roof curving up and all sorts of painted carvings of animals and birds decorating it. Everything around it—sidewalks, buildings, a huge empty plaza—looks new, like someone built them yesterday.

"It's like the whole country's being renovated," Dad says. "A construction site. And what they're putting up

…" he shook his head. "You'd think they'd want to keep more of the beautiful old stuff."

"Especially after the Cultural Revolution," Mom adds. I ask what that is. "It was this craziness that a small group in the government started in the sixties. They decided that everything that had to do with culture or education, beauty, anything about the past, had to be destroyed. And the people connected to those things like teachers, artists—or who they thought were connected to them—were humiliated, beaten, imprisoned, even killed. And I think the survivors lost ties to many of their traditions."

I realize there's a whole load of things I don't know. I wonder if even Sam knows stuff like that about China.

Before we get the babies, we need one final approval from the government, so we make a stop at the notary's office, another boring two-story building. As we step off the bus, a group of young men calls out to us, "Hello, hello." Mom waves and shouts, "*Ni hao!*" The men laugh and give her a thumbs-up.

Jing Jing brings us into a waiting room and then we take turns in the toilet. When I finally get in there, I'm in shock. There's just an opening in the tile floor. The floor around it is wet, and I don't want to think about why. There's no toilet paper, and I'm glad I don't need any. I think about the restaurant in Chinatown that bothered Olivia. I could only imagine what she'd say about this. I guess, like Meredith told her, it's just that different people find different things important.

The notary is this mean-looking lady sitting behind a desk. She barks out some questions for Mom and Dad. Jing Jing translates: Will they take care of their baby forever? Educate her? Teach her about her Chinese heritage? Mom and Dad answer "Yes" each time. I can tell they've both teared up. Then the woman asks what the baby's English name will be. We had talked about that a lot. Mom tells her, barely getting the words out, "Lily Isabelle." Lily for Cousin Lil. Isabelle for Isaac.

The woman nods, signs something, and signals we can leave. And that's that. We are cleared for takeoff.

The whole group heads back onto the bus, and we drive over to the orphanage. An Rui had told us that these places aren't exactly called orphanages. The Chinese words translate more like "social welfare yard." Maybe that's because the word orphanage sounds just as bad in Chinese as it does in English.

The "yard" turns out to be a new, bright and shiny white building with five floors. It's ugly, but nothing at all like the dark, old, creepy places orphanages are made out to be in movies or books. Jing Jing points to the smaller, older building right next to it and tells us that's where the orphanage had been before the new one went up. It's being used as an old-age home now. It's actually nice, more old-fashioned and my idea of Chinese-looking. There's only two stories, with balconies on the second floor that overlook a courtyard. In the middle of the courtyard is a statue. I walk closer to see what it's a stature of. And I can't believe it. It's Kwan Yin. She is sitting on a humongous flower, one arm around a small child, who's looking up at her with a big-ass smile. It makes me think of Mom. And, for some reason, Owen.

Everyone else has gone inside the new building, and I'm still out here with Kwan Yin. Mom comes over to me.

"Are you all right?"

"Yeah. I just like the statue." I don't know how to tell her what it means to me. I just say, "It's like one I saw in the museum."

Mom's eyes widen. "The museum? What museum? When did you—" She shakes her head. "We'll talk about that later." Then she takes my arm and we walk over to Dad, who's waiting at the front door. The other families are already inside, seated on high-backed chairs in a big room with red-painted walls.

Mr. Li, the director of the orphanage, walks in. He's a small man, dressed in a suit and tie. He takes a seat in the center of the room and proceeds to talk. And talk. Jing Jing can't keep up with him. She translates as much of what he's saying as she can. Mostly he's going on about how smart all the babies are, how fat, and how well he has cared for them. I hope he's right. He probably is. Jing Jing has told us that the fact that we're here at all, inside the orphanage, means that the authorities are proud of it.

I look around at the other people in our group. They all are nodding at the director, smiles frozen on their faces, trying to be polite. But I know they're tired, hungry, and so anxious to get their babies they can barely sit still. Well, at least that's how I feel. I can see, right outside the door, the nannies, wearing white coats, waiting, holding the babies. We can hear crying. Finally, Mr. Li decides it's time to let the nannies come in.

I turn to Mom. "It's your last chance. We could just go home and get one of Crazy Harold's dogs instead."

She laughs. "I don't think so." She looks at me and then gives me a kiss. "I love you so much."

"I know, Mom," I answer. "Me too."

The nannies come through the door, each carrying a baby dressed in the same striped outfit. One by one they hand the babies to Mr. Li. Everyone knows their child immediately, and rushes up to get her before the director can call their names. Then Mr. Li passes the baby on to the family. It reminds me a little of Hallie handing out stickers that day at Mom's school.

And that starts me thinking—what if we are given a dragonfly instead of a ladybug or a butterfly? What would that mean? Handing out kids like that—actual human beings. The whole thing is too strange and crazy and amazing. These Chinese kids are being given to Americans. What will that make them? Chinese? American? All mixed up? Never sure of themselves, like Sean?

And what about the poor little thing we're about to get? What's the end game for her? Getting us as a family? Me as a brother? A kid who so wasn't ready to be somebody else's brother? I'm Isaac's brother. Isn't that who I am?

But Mom is smiling like she's going to burst, and Dad is already behind the video camera. For a second I think I might scream, *Stop! What are you doing?* Then I realize it'll sound really bad on the tape.

Mom is heading for Mr. Li. I follow her, Dad filming it all. Mr. Li is saying something to the nanny. The baby's tiny nose is running. Mom takes a tissue from her purse and wipes it. The director smiles and says something else. Something with the word "mama." And now Mom is holding the baby.

"Hello, little one," she says. "Hello, Lily Isabelle. *Ni hao, xiao* Lil. *Wo shi ni di mama.* It's going to be all right."

I see the baby's eyes following Mom's face, like she's trying to learn it. She and Mom already belong to each other. I feel the tears come.

"Here, your turn," Mom tells Dad. They exchange baby and camera. Dad says, "Hi, Lily," and he starts to do a slow waltz with the baby, singing some old song with her name in it, about how a love song is a sad song. A song of woe.

He stops in front of me.

"Do you want to hold her, A-Team?" Dad's question is filled with love, sorrow, happiness, hope.

I hold out my arms, and Dad places the bundle that is my sister into them. I look at her. "Hey." She doesn't make a sound as her eyes search my face. I smile. "Wait till we get you home," I say. "Everybody's waiting to meet you." I lean in to give her a kiss.

That's from Isaac, I tell her silently.

THE END

Made in the USA
Lexington, KY
18 July 2013